ASCENT OF A VENGEFUL WOMAN

UNCOVERED DARKNESS SERIES
BOOK TWO

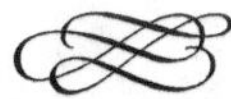

ASHON RUFFINS

Copyright © 2023 by Dreadful Times Press, LLC

Edited by:

Chelsea Terry - Stand Corrected Editing

Nichole Heydenburg - Poisoned Ink Press

Roxana Coumans - Roth Notions

Cover Design by Fay Lane Graphic Design

ISBN 979-8-9855902-3-4

First printing 2023

DEDICATION

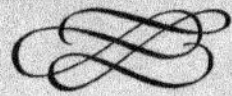

To K.A.T.
The journey continues.

CHAPTER 1

2⁰⁰⁹

15 YEARS after the events of Goliath

THE COOL NEW ORLEANS air filled my lungs as I pursued the shadow that moved swiftly down the cramped alleyway off of Saint Peter Street. The boisterous laughter and music of the neighboring clubs on Bourbon Street were an inadequate distraction as I fixated on the nimble movement of the black-cloaked figure ahead, obscured under the darkness of the night. My legs fatigued from the weight of my freshly shined Army boots as I struggled to maintain pace with Carlos. His taunting, bellowing laughter echoed off the wood of the timeworn buildings as the chase continued down another, even more narrow, alleyway. I slowed, my chest constricted, gasping for air as I leaned against the wooden exterior of the building next to me. The stale and pungent odor of its rotting wood burned the inside of my nostrils.

"Come on, Nola. You can do better than that." The glee of Carlos' voice was clear as his mocking echoed in the night air.

"You've murdered your last woman, Carlos," I yelled.

I raised and pointed the revolver in my hand. Its onyx plating shimmered off the alleyway lights as I pulled the trigger. The flash of fire and thunderous sound of the discharged bullets gave chase to Carlos at the other end.

Carlos crashed through a nearby door. His unnatural strength splintered it to pieces as the bullets ricocheted off the nearby brick in the corner of the entryway. His eerie laughter continued to echo as he fled deeper into the darkness of the abandoned building. I slowed as I followed behind him. The depths of the darkness forced me to squint as I tried to adjust to the lack of light inside. The physical struggle to suppress the sound of my labored breaths caused frustration. Even as subtle as they were, I knew it was loud enough to give away my position inside. I inhaled deeply and gently exhaled to gather my control. A smirk presented itself on my face as I raised my gun once again.

"What's the matter, Carlos? You don't want to play with me? I know you can smell me. My sweat. My peach blossom scented lotion. Don't I smell appealing to you? I'm sure you've been wanting to taste my blood for some time now." I said. My heart thumped with excitement at the thrill of this hunt. The challenge of a lioness as it stalked its prey.

"Oh, Nola, you do smell sweet. I'm sure you taste even sweeter. Tempt me all you want, child, but I won't make this easy for you by giving in to my ego," Carlos replied. His voice sounded as if it came from the multitude of rooms surrounding me.

The building appeared to be an abandoned home built almost a century ago. Like so many others in the French Quarter area of New Orleans, the French colonial architecture had a large open area in the center, surrounded by chipped and faded green colored doors. The dank stench of mold filled the air.

"Don't tell me you're scared of a little girl, Carlos. What are you, 200 years old? Your vicious reputation as a vampire didn't include any tales of a sniveling coward," I yelled.

The smirk on my face grew more present as I cleared hallway after hallway. The rigid grid design of the barrel of my revolver led the way, while I attempted to bait him out.

Rapid footsteps quickly approached behind me. The sound of the creepy bellowing laugh was more abundant as I turned and was struck in the ribs by the quick blow of Carlos' fist. A blur of a figure as he passed. I stumbled back onto the floor and fired another round, hitting Carlos on the shoulder as I slid several feet across the dusty wooden floor from his assault. His strike prevented a proper aim. Carlos laughed harder.

"Nola Maor, the heroic hunter. Appears the tales of you are exaggerated. Maybe before I bleed you, I can add to that pretty little scar on your face."

I climbed to my feet and tracked Carlos' voice once again. Sadly, wounding a vampire served no purpose but to piss them off. They didn't bleed, and anything short of piercing the heart or exposing them to sunlight was ineffective—a futile exercise in violence. Every movie and piece of fiction I knew had it wrong. Vampires weren't pretty. They weren't misunderstood. Holy water and garlic didn't do a damn thing but get the uninformed slaughtered. The only thing that worked was either silver or wood through the heart. That would put one of these parasites down for good.

"That was your chance, Carlos, and you missed." I shouted, glancing down at my hunting companion and counted the remaining silver forged rounds in its barrel. "Tell me, how many of your kind have I put down over the years? About a dozen or so, right? Maybe I've dusted a couple of your longtime friends."

From the corner of the room, Carlos stepped out of the darkness. His eyes glowed blood red, and his jagged teeth mirrored that of a piranha. His dried, cracked skin looked as if it was worn leather assaulted by years in a desert heat. Carlos hissed as he flickered his grotesque split tongue in my direction. The sight of him was revolting. I could only smirk at the thought of the romanticized depictions of vampires often found in Hollywood movies. There was nothing appealing about this bloodthirsty predator. If my aim wasn't up to par, I would fall like the many souls Carlos' hive had already consumed. Deaths I could have prevented.

"I'm going to enjoy this, girl," Carlos said as he moved closer out of the darkness.

My heart thumped with anticipation at the sight of him. The thrill could only be compared to a hunter in the woods finally having a clear shot at the elusive bear he had been hunting for years. The wooden boards creaked under stress closer to the center of the room. I pulled the silver-plated dagger from my waistband with a free hand, then hurled it at Carlos's heart. Carlos moved swiftly, evaded the dagger, latched onto the drywall with cat-like movement, and ran along the wall parallel to the ground. His razor-sharp nails pulled away pieces of dry wall as he moved on all fours and circled my position. The onyx plated .44 caliber Magnum revolver, affectionally named Corbin, raised to eye level and tracked Carlos. His sharp nails ripped the dry wall to pieces as he crawled along, making his way closer to me.

Carlos leaped from the wall, with his long, sharp fingernails extended. Before his sharpened fangs could get close, I fired. The silver round ripped through his dead heart. The lifeless body fell to the floor. The skin sizzled and smoked, and its flesh melted away as if dowsed with acid. Only the charred bone remained.

With Corbin snuggled safely back into my shoulder holster—the brown leather heated from the barrel smelled of the oil used to maintain the holster's healthy disposition—I walked near the remains of Carlos.

"I wish I could have found you sooner. A lot fewer people would have died." I lifted my boot and stomped the skull of the once elusive predator and shattered it to pieces.

I pulled the thick plastic trash bag from my back pant pocket and shook it open, placing Carlos' brittle charred bones inside.

Flashing blue light pierced the window of the abandoned building and illuminated the room I stood in.

"Shit, NOPD is here."

I made my way back to the splintered doorway and exhaled with relief as I gazed upon a familiar face.

"Detective Jordan, I'm glad it's you."

"Hey, Nola. On the hunt again?" Jordan asked.

"Vampire. I think that was the last of a hive left in the city. The department should have fewer missing people cases to investigate for a while. How did you know something was going down in this alleyway?"

"The gunshots were called in by a citizen. No witnesses. Just reported hearing the shots close by. At least the citizens are still calling and not apathetic to the gun violence. This time of night, my instincts were telling me it was you, but you know this city. I couldn't be sure."

"I should have known someone heard the shots fired. This city never sleeps, except to sleep off hangovers on Sunday mornings, maybe." I smirked.

"Per usual with the vamps, nothing left but charred bones, right?" Jordan questioned.

"Yeah, I'll take care of it. The bones are pretty brittle now, anyway. Easily shattered and easily bagged," I said as I pointed to the plastic sack over my shoulder. "You can just advise dispatch that it's a 21-Unfounded incident, nothing or no one was out here on your arrival. Not even your brass has to know about this. It's not like they'll pay me for it, anyway." I laughed.

Jordan smiled at me and nodded in approval. He pointed at the trickle of blood that slid down my arm.

"Oh, I didn't know that was there. Damn vamp kicked up some drywall in the fight. A piece must have nicked me."

"You know, Nola, the department hasn't been the same since you left. Any chance you would come back and be a part of the team again? Homicide could use you."

"Not a chance! I can't hunt these things and be under the thumb of the department. Once Goliath showed his ugly face, it sounded the alarm and emboldened all these creatures to reveal themselves. Someone must deal with the uncovered darkness within this world. Unfortunately, there aren't many hunters like me and my sister out there. Besides, I remember our time in the First Precinct homicide together. You could handle yourself back then, and all these years later, you can handle yourself now. I'm sure the department is safe in your hands. I have to wonder, though, still working overnight homicides?"

"What about it?"

"I could use a partner. Someone I trust. Besides, knowing these things exist is most of the early struggle with this job. Hunting them opens your eyes to a much bigger picture of the world," I said, a rare smile present as I tried to entice my former colleague.

"Maybe. I still feel like there is some good I can do right where I am. Look, it's been fifteen years since Goliath tore this city apart. People haven't forgotten, but they're forgetting. So are the NOPD leadership. All of that happened a few mayors ago. Either you're doing a fantastic job hunting these monsters or people are becoming ignorant of the things going on around them again, or even worse, apathetic. There are less reported sightings of the supernatural these days. You know how things are once shit gets inconvenient. I'd hate to see NOPD or City Hall hang you out to dry."

"No need to worry about me. There isn't much I fear anymore. Politics and politicians are the least of my worries. Hell, the more I think about it, maybe it would be best if everyone forgot what was out there. Maybe the old normal is what this city needs. The rest of the country is doing a pretty damn good job of forgetting."

"I don't know. Sounds above my pay grade. Whatever is needed, I'm glad you're on our side." Detective Jordan smiled. His gaze lingered on me as he took a deep breath. "Nola, on a side note, do you mind if I give you a call sometime? Or maybe we can just go out and have a couple of drinks and not talk about some of the more gruesome things going on? You know, we could focus on some of the beauty this world has to offer."

His handsome yet smooth complexion and bright smile still appealed to me. It didn't seem that long ago Jordan was a rookie Homicide Detective working overnights.

"Maybe. The answer isn't no, but right now, there is still work to be done. I have to drive this sack of bones out of town to a mortuary that disposes of this type of carcass." I stared into his light brown eyes as he looked back at me with a crooked smile. "Maybe I'll give you a call sometime this week and take you up on that drink."

"You do that."

CHAPTER 2

The drive down the spacious road of the small town's Main Street provoked a smile on Ms. Jones's face, even with the unwelcomed stares that greeted them from the peculiar-looking townspeople upon her and Tammy's arrival into town. Ms. Jones couldn't help but feel overjoyed at the potentially unprecedented real-estate project she was about to sink her teeth into. The rundown old town was dilapidated and only fifty miles or so outside of Nashville, Tennessee. It took on a lot of the nearby city's temperament but retained its unfriendly attitude to outsiders like plenty of small towns in the South. The sporadic yet prominent displays of Confederate flags decorated outside the few businesses still in operation reminded Ms. Jones exactly where she had driven from the Nashville airport. The formidable forest that isolated the town from the surrounding cities allowed the residents to keep their backward way of thinking.

Despite Ms. Jones's excitement, the continual sight of the repulsive blue X with the embedded stars and red background mounted in the windows of the struggling businesses and boarded up abandoned buildings instilled a sense of nausea in her belly. Ms. Jones rolled down the passenger side window and allowed the rush of cold air into the car. Her shoulder length hair moved slightly with the wind's gentle touch. Ms. Jones's brown lipstick matched the umber tone of her well pampered and smooth skin. The blue blouse she wore under her designer gray skirt suit had the top two buttons unfastened. Alone in the car with Tammy as she drove, it allowed for a more relaxed environment. If this were a corporate meeting, Ms. Jones' wardrobe style would have been played differently.

"Ms. Jones, we're both New Yorkers, but twenty-five-degree air is just as uncomfortable in Tennessee as it is in New York. Do you mind putting the window back up, ma'am?" Tammy, Ms. Jones' Executive Assistant, pushed the pink square frames of her glasses back firmly on the bridge of her thin nose with the tip of her index finger.

Ms. Jones glared over at Tammy as she pulled at the top button of her blouse to ensure it was secured again. Tammy's sense of style always confused Ms. Jones. Often dressed conservatively in a completely buttoned blouse and loose ankle length skirt, Tammy's make-up usually comprised of bright colors. Her choice for the trip to Dalyville, Tennessee—pink cream lipstick with pastel blue eye shadow. Not very conservative.

"Sorry about that. You know, I've sat across some of the most ruthless men in New York and have brokered multi-million-dollar real-estate deals without one bead of sweat on my brow, but the sight of that flag still gets a rise out of me. The cold air helped with anger," Ms. Jones said.

"This town should be happy you're here, ma'am. The things you have planned will be beneficial to them and their families. They will then have to reconcile with their old-fashion way of thinking when things improve for them," Tammy replied.

"Tammy, you've been around long enough to know that's a very naïve perspective."

Tammy pursed her thin lips and rolled her sky-blue colored eyes as she pulled into one of the empty parking spaces in front of the antiquated Sheriff's Department. The building, much like the rest of the town, appeared to be barely standing. The old wooden structure looked every bit of the years it probably had to survive abuse at the hands of mother nature's storms and the brutal test of father time. Along with planks of wooden siding, it was missing the obvious sign needed to advise to the small town of fifty people what was inside. Apparently, it wasn't needed for such a small population. After both Ms. Jones and Tammy stepped out of their car, the door to the sheriff's station opened. A rather large burly man with a full salt-and-pepper beard, wearing a snug fitting sheriff's uniform stepped out. He nodded at the ladies, while he pulled at the brim of his large, circular sheriff's hat. His pale skin was highlighted by the slight red in his cheeks after the contact with the cold air.

"You must be Ms. Ashley Jones. I'm Sheriff Paul Alfred. Welcome to Dalyville, Tennessee. It's a pleasure to finally meet you. Your representatives have been in and out of this town, buying up property for quite a while. It's good to finally put a face with the name."

"Hello, Sheriff Alfred, it's a pleasure," Ms. Jones said, stepping forward to shake his hand. She stepped back and gestured to Tammy, still looking at the officer. "This is my assistant, Ms. Tammy Hodges. I'm happy to finally get down here and visit the properties in person. I've had my project manager down here a couple of times in my place. I'm sure you've met him."

"I've heard of another feller from New York that came through here, but I hadn't had the pleasure of meeting him," Sheriff Alfred said. His smile was bright, and his gaze lingered in Tammy's direction before he looked back at Ms. Jones. "Well, I want to warn you there are a lot of people here that are not too happy with you and what you have planned. I understand what you're trying to do, and I know it would do a lot of good for this town and for the African American community in Nashville as a whole, but the ones who haven't sold to you have plans to fight you and your investors, tooth and nail, ma'am."

"Sheriff, I've been a land developer for a long time, a little more than twenty years, in fact, and I see you've done your research on me. Yes, most of my partners happen to be black, and all have the plans of bringing tech businesses to this area. We're talking about jobs, banks, housing, grocery stores, partnerships with surrounding universities and eventually a new university for tech and engineering students. It's not about our color, but a chance to build something the entire state of Tennessee can be proud of," Ms. Jones replied.

Sheriff Alfred walked toward his police car. He peered over the top of it and stared at Ms. Jones and Tammy. The smile on his face was bright, as if he just listened to a sibling give him a speech that made him proud. Tammy stared back with a slight blush on her pale cheeks.

"Ma'am, I couldn't agree with you more. Your color doesn't matter. This town needs every bit of what you and your investors are trying to do here. I'll do everything in my power to make sure things go smoothly. Now, I know why you've made the trip and what you've come to see. Let's get goin' before we lose sunlight. I don't want to be out there after dark."

THE SHORT DRIVE outside of the main part of town as they followed behind the sheriff led Ms. Jones and Tammy down a narrow, grassy, and rock graveled road. It was as though the worn track was once a clear path that had been taken back by nature. The wind howled as it cut through the tight knitting of trees, as if the wintered forest was infested with the screams of unnatural creatures. The brake lights of the sheriff's car illuminated and added a red hue to the already gloomy atmosphere. Both cars pulled into the large, open crescent-shaped field.

Seven aged wooden structures lined the outside of the area which gave it its crescent shape. Each minuscule building was designed and built in the exact same way, like an unimaginatively designed suburb that infested the land outside major cities today. The structures were nothing more than single-family homes. All were built with triangular shaped roofing and a wooden front porch the length of the front of the homes. The porch was centered with stairs in front and a single window on the left front side of the door. A thick, tree-lined forest stood directly behind it all, blocking out the sun and feeding into the gloomy atmosphere.

"My God, this is creepy! It's almost as if the sun doesn't shine here," Ms. Jones said.

A crimson-colored brick constructed well centered the area. The brick matched the type and color of brick used to build the chimneys of each home. The well was a bit different. The wooden cover and winding crank with the rope and bucket was missing from the standard design. Only the jagged edges of two wooden poles on each side of the well protruded from the brick on the top.

"Ladies, welcome to the original 1830 Irish settlement of Dalyville," Sheriff Alfred said with a bit of a smug tone and a crooked forced smile.

"So, this is the area that came with the Glendale property?" Ms. Jones asked, her brow curled as she stared at Tammy.

"A small oversight by the townspeople, ma'am. Instead of the property owned by the town itself, the property lines of the Glendale's included this settlement. A small oversight by the town, I'm sure, but one that was beneficial in your favor, ma'am," Tammy said.

"This is a stunning piece of land. Creepy, but stunning. It's like stepping back in time. The description from the Gallagher's journal in the Tennessee state archives doesn't do it justice. Tammy, remind me to thank Charles for such a fine job."

Tammy cut her eyes away from Ms. Jones, quickly turned her head, and slowly exhaled.

"I will ma'am." Tammy mumbled.

"Charles?" the Sheriff inquired.

"Charles is her Property Acquisition Scout and Project Manager. He scouts potential properties Ms. Jones may be interested in," Tammy replied.

"Sheriff, I see the town still takes pride in this place. The area's landscaping is almost perfect."

"Well, see now, that's the funny part. No one comes up here. There are about fifty people that live in this town and every one of them avoids this place."

"Then how does…"

"How does the area's landscape stay maintained? It doesn't, Ms. Jones," the Sheriff interrupted. He walked closer to both Ms. Jones and Tammy and inhaled deeply. His hands rubbed together as he turned and looked at the well in the center of the settlement. "Nothin' grows out here. Nothin' grows and nothin' changes color with the seasons. Some strange things happened here."

"What do you mean, strange things?" Tammy raised her brow.

"Strange things!" he shouted anxiously as he removed his large-brimmed hat and stared down at it in his hands. His voice once again settled down to a calmer tone. "Look, Ms. Jones, like I told you before, the town knows about your development plans. Aside from the ones who have sold out to you and your partners, the others don't want you here. Is your skin color a problem? Yes. Would the fact that you're an outsider, in general, be a problem? Yes, a bigger problem. We only have one black family that lives here. The fact that you're from New York doesn't make this situation any better, either. Ma'am, most importantly, the people who don't plan on selling don't want you to touch this place. They just want you to leave, immediately, before you make things worse around here."

"Make things worse around here? Strange occurrences? This is the most pathetic attempt I've ever encountered. I'm not going to abandon this project, not for a few angry townspeople and definitely not for half-baked cryptic danger warnings," Ms. Jones said, pulling her silver highlighted colored hair back behind her ear. "Sheriff, you seem like a good person. You can choose to keep up with this superstitious nonsense or not. Whatever you decide, you and your fellow townspeople should know that this development plan is going to happen. It's too important of a project, and it can help a lot of people in this state."

Ms. Jones turned and stomped the few feet back to the car. Tammy was only steps behind her.

"That's your choice, ma'am. I agree with you on the need. Just know that the people 'round here won't like it. They won't like it one bit," the sheriff mumbled.

"That's their problem, Sheriff. Right now, all I want to do is go back to my shitty motel and get out of this cold weather. Tammy, I want to come back tomorrow and tour the structures. They may be worth preserving, or maybe I can make them into office space. This area could be the location for the new university. The town deserves that, at least."

"Yes, ma'am," Tammy answered. She turned to face the sheriff, as she jotted notes down in her phone for Ms. Jones. "Lead the way, Sheriff Alfred."

The sheriff smiled at Tammy as she walked to the driver's side door and turned toward him.

"In my opinion, sheriff, this settlement is an old relic of a controversial past in direct conflict with the promising outlook of a bright future. It's not worth keeping around," Tammy said, her brow raised as she pointed toward the old structures.

"Yes, ma'am."

CHAPTER 3

Oil popped out of the frying pan and splattered the stove as the sizzling turkey bacon charred around the edges and its aroma, along with the freshly brewed coffee, filled the modest sized kitchen in Janice's home. Although she could go toe-to-toe with almost any manner of beast in a darkened alley, the fine aspects of the culinary arts were monsters Janice never learned to slay. She moved frantically around the kitchen's island as she plated the food she prepared early that Monday morning. A silver crucifix dangled from her neck as she spruced the assorted fruit on the plates set out earlier on the kitchen table. The crucifix was a symbol of victory. Janice and Nola purchased the twin set necklaces after Nola's battle with Goliath. Her smile, almost ever present on her face, lingered as she heard the tapping of multiple footsteps behind her.

"Hey, mama," Jackson said, giving his mother a quick peck on her cheek. A single gesture that helped maintain that smile on her face each morning.

"Good morning, son," Janice replied.

"Good morning, hon," Darrius walked up behind her and kissed Janice on the other cheek as they both sat at the kitchen table. The kiss from Darrius sparked a unique set of feelings from within Janice.

"Good morning, baby. Breakfast is on the table for you. You earned it last night," Janice whispered in Darrius' ear with a crooked smirk on her face.

She wrapped her arms around his waist and squeezed his charcoal gray tailored suit, placing the side of her face firmly onto his chest and against his blue silk tie. Janice was always a fan of Darrius' tall, lean, athletic frame he managed to maintain since his college years.

"Ew, mama! I heard that." Jackson mimicked a gag as he covered his mouth with his hand and sat at the table.

A burst of laughter erupted from Janice and Darrius.

"How'd my fellas sleep last night?"

"We're good. Ready for school and ready for work. My schedule is a little tight today. I have a meeting with a potential client that would be big for the firm. Jackson and I will have to leave a little earlier this morning to drive into Nashville," Darrius stated. His eyes widened as he scarfed down the food in front of him, as if he had not eaten in days.

Janice looked over at Jackson and watched as her thinly built son completely devoured every speck of food on his plate. It was as if the boy was a black hole of all things savory. She could only smile when she looked at Jackson's big brown eyes and curly, mini afro.

"Okay, let's get you boys out of here so you can take care of your business. I have some things on the agenda as well." Janice took a couple of quick bites of turkey bacon.

She and Darrius stood from the table and put their dishes away after they quickly devoured the remaining portions on their plates on their way to the kitchen.

"Eat it now, taste it later," Darrius said as he laughed.

Darrius adjusted his tie and guzzled his orange juice without coming up for air. Janice walked toward him, already removing his coat from the closet door beside him.

"Honey, does the bureau have a case or something for you? You look like you're on the clock, so to speak," Darrius asked.

"Darrius, I'm retired. The bureau can have what they want. I'm only here for you guys. Any cases I work, I work on my own— as a hunter and not an agent."

"Okay, I get it, but why the urgency for today? It's not like there's much to do around here," Darrius inquired.

"I know. It's just that the developer who's been buying up land is in town, and it sounds like she already visited the settlement from the information the sheriff gave me. Things could get out of hand real soon if the mayor gets involved. I just need to speak to her, or at the minimum, debrief the sheriff after I meet with her and tell her what's going on around here," Janice replied.

"Ah, good ol' Sheriff Alfred. That's a pretty cool white guy. I feel like if he wasn't a cop, he would be in somebody's rock band. I get drummer vibes from him." Darrius smirked as he played a set of air drums and bobbed his head like a rocker.

"Why are you like this?" Janice laughed, yanking playfully at his favorite blue tie.

"Seriously, do you think something is about to go down?" Darrius said. His playful tone was a little weightier, placing his hand on Janice's shoulder.

"I'm not sure, but my instincts are telling me something is about to happen. We've been here fifteen years, and I haven't gotten any solid evidence of what the hell is going on out at that settlement or in this town. I didn't gain much ground, even with the resources the bureau gave me. Either the sheriff is completely in the dark with what is going on with all the missing people as well, or there are some fairly powerful forces at work here that I haven't quite figured out yet," Janice said.

Jackson stood from the table and finished his orange juice. Janice noticed him leering at her from across the room; his face contorted in confusion.

"Whatever is going on, I hope you can close this out, mama. I'm ready to leave this place. It's so boring. And they don't want us here," Jackson said.

"Sweetheart, you know how this goes. We don't leave until whatever it is we're hunting is either destroyed or captured."

"I know, mama. I know. We gotta go, Dad," Jackson concluded.

Janice looked at both her son and her husband in the eyes and could only smile at the strength they showed. This was the only home Jackson had ever known, and Darrius always had the desire to move back home to New Orleans.

"Okay, Jackson. You know the routine. Back here after school. First, homework. Second, we study the hunt. Last, we train. You got it? We need to work on your defense." Janice punched Jackson on the shoulder firmly, her bright smile still ever present.

"Shit, mama, can't we take a break for one day? I promise I'll make up for it on Saturday." Jackson sighed heavily, as he rubbed his shoulder.

"Excuse me! Jackson, that's no way for a fifteen-year-old boy to talk to his mother. You'll pay for that later in training," Darrius replied.

"Yes, Dad. I'm sorry, mama," Jackson replied earnestly.

"It's okay, son. Do you guys have your kits in your bags? Crucifix, silver-plated pen, small iron rods lining your belts, and salt?" Janice pulled at her son's belt and checked her husband's bag. "I suppose you should have your lunches too," she said, smiling and handing both their lunch bags.

"Honey, we have everything. We've trained with you and have prepared as you taught us. We love you, but we gotta go. What's on your agenda today, anyway?" Darrius walked out the door, toward the car.

Janice followed. Jackson had already anxiously opened his car door and sat inside.

"I told you, babe, that developer is in town. I have to try to speak with her about her plans for the original settlement. My investigation still hasn't pinpointed what's bubbling under the surface out there, but it's something, and it's dangerous. I have to try to steer her away from it."

"That's right. Sorry, I forgot just that fast. Okay, well… good luck. I love you," Darrius said. His lips gently touched Janice's. She repaid the gesture. Grabbed him by the tie, and pulled him towards her, planting a firmer kiss on him.

"I love you too, baby."

Janice made her way back inside and leaned against the door, her head tilted slightly back. Her thoughts deep in worry for the two most important people in her life. Her focus shifted as she sighed, consumed with a nagging feeling that she needed to keep both Jackson and Darrius unharmed.

Janice shook her head quickly, regained her focus, and rushed to her makeshift personal library. When the Federal Bureau of Investigation set her up with this house after she was assigned to Dalyville, she made the main bedroom—the second largest room in the house, her library. She didn't regret buying it from the bureau or making the room all hers. It was her favorite room in the house. It was her place, and one of the few places Janice felt at ease. An earthy smell fixed inside because of the comprehensive collection of books that lined the bookshelves and eventually stacked on the floor after she exhausted the shelf space. Even when she didn't have a case to investigate or some supernatural entity to hunt, she found herself in there occasionally to escape the frequent madness of living with a Type A personality husband and a teenage son.

Relics of past closed cases, and every type of weapon needed to hunt any manner of beast or apparition, accompanied the books and littered the shelves and racks. As a child, Janice could have never imagined she would end up as part of a fringe division in the FBI. Her parents were practical devout Catholics. Raised in that type of environment, Janice could only see herself in a practical profession. In her eyes, there was nothing more practical and more serving than becoming a federal agent. It was her outstanding performance as a cadet and an agent that opened doors for her at the FBI. Eventually, proving herself as capable and trustworthy, which opened the door for the fringe division assignment. The division that opened her eyes to the unknown world around her.

Janice sat on the floor and stared at the many faces on the missing persons' flyers. Her knuckles whitened as she tightened her grip on the pen in frustration. The dates on the posters ranged over a span of twenty years, and the victims had few commonalities. The only thing Janice had noticed was the timespan people started going missing was after the last farm went under—around the same time things had become a little tougher here. The townsfolk were a lot angrier.

The violent rattle of the vibrating cell phone against the wooden floorboard impeded her focus. Janice inhaled sharply, closed her eyes, and slowly exhaled before she answered.

"Hello, little sis," she said, her voice monotone and barely present.

The smile Janice had all morning was nowhere to be found. The phone fell silent for a few brief seconds before she spoke.

"Hey, Janice. H-how are things?"

"Things are fine, Nola. We're fine. It's been a while since we talked."

Another long silence followed between them after the dry greetings.

"How is the private investigation lifestyle treating you?" Janice followed.

"I just put down a master vampire a couple of days ago, but the other side of the business that pays the bills has been a little slow," Nola replied.

"It's been slow for me here, too. I was assigned here fifteen years ago and I'm still trying to figure out where these people went. The only thing I've figured out is that they usually disappear after visiting the original settlement. It's the last place they were seen, but that settlement doesn't have one speck of blood or one board out of place. Nothing but trash left over from makeshift parties. My research has found the town has a lot of deep and disturbing history associated with it, but nothing so far to tie it to anything unnatural going on today," Janice said. Her tone picked up as it usually did when she talked hunter shop.

"Whatever it is, big sis, I'm sure you'll figure it out. From what you've told me, it's not a big town, I'm sure whatever supernatural force is causing it, it will slip up soon. If it's supernatural," Nola stated, then exhaled sharply before she continued. "Come to think of it, Janice, before everything happened with Mom and Dad, we talked all the time. Years ago, you said there was an energy, something unnatural there that might have something to do with that town's history. I know you said it was just a hunch, but your instincts are usually spot on. You just have to find the source. Find the source, and you'll figure out what's taking those people."

The phone fell silent for several moments. Janice stared at the screen of her cell phone. Her heart thumped in her chest as the anger boiled over inside her. She set the phone down on the floor; her index finger activated the speakerphone.

"Janice. Janice, are you there?" Nola asked. Her voice cracked as she called out.

"Nola, why did you have to bring them up? We were doing fine, talking shop and using what we do to connect a little. You had to mention them, didn't you?" Janice's hands trembled and her eyes welled.

"Because I miss them. I miss them so much. I know it's been years, but don't you miss them? It hurts so much," Nola cried.

"Don't you fucking say that to me! Of course, I miss them. Mom and Dad didn't deserve what happened to them. It's all your fault! You took them from me. You should have been doing your fucking job. You are in New Orleans. It was your responsibility. They were your responsibility!" Janice screamed at the phone. Her eyes were swollen and red, and tears fell down her cheeks.

"It wasn't my fault. The thing got away from me. It figured out who they were and where they lived. By the time I found it, it was too late."

"Damn right, it was too late. You were careless, and you under-estimated it because you took down Goliath. Now my parents are dead. Their throats ripped out by a fucking lycanthrope while they slept. We needed them, Nola. We needed them," Janice continued to cry.

"J-Janice, I fought it. I tried to kill it. I don't know what type of werewolf it was, but it was strong, unusually strong. It almost appeared as though the silver didn't affect the damn thing. It nearly killed me, and it left me with a scar to remind me about it every day I look into a mirror. I've been looking. I've been looking for it all these years, and I promise I'll find it. I'm sorry. I'm so sorry. If I could fix it, I would. I—"

"Sorry? Fuck, you're sorry. You can't fix it. Just like you said, you have a nice scar on your face to remind you every day of what you did. I hate you," Janice yelled.

"Sis, you don't mean that. You don't mean that, Janice. I love y —" Nola said as Janice ended the call.

Her tears were plentiful. Her hands gripped and pulled at her blouse near her chest as if the pain was unbearable.

Janice kicked the papers laying on the floor and pushed over a nearby stack of books. She wiped the tears away as they fell from her eyes. Janice focused on a single photograph, which turned over after her brief display of frustration. The well in the center of the original settlement of town was the focus of the photo. She had looked down that well dozens of times during search missions with local law enforcement every time someone went missing. Hell, she had searched every shack standing in the crescent-shaped settlement and the wooded area surrounding it. Nothing. Nothing but the story of its past and the eerie feeling that came over you when you stepped foot into the area.

"Just like the pain that place brought in the past, it's bringing that same pain now," she mumbled.

Janice's phone once again illuminated and rattled on the floor as if she just had a brilliant revelation. It was a phone call.

"God, don't be her." She peeked over at the screen, exhaling with relief. "Sheriff Alfred, how are you doing today? To what do I owe this phone call?"

"Special Agent Williams, you wanted me to inform you when the investor came to town. You were right—not sure how you knew she was coming—but she showed up here. Came into town yesterday. Her name is Ashley Jones. She brought her assistant with her as well. Her name is Tammy Hodges. Ms. Jones is a bit of a firecracker. You know they won't like that 'round here," the sheriff stated firmly.

"Paul, I've been down here for fifteen years, only a couple of years before you became the sheriff. Since your predecessor passed away, you're the only one who knows who I am and why I'm here. Plus, we are pretty good friends, I think. For the love of God, please call me Janice."

The last thing Janice wanted was for anyone to accidentally hear the word agent while in the townsfolk's company.

"You're right. Well, I called to let you know that Ms. Jones and Ms. Hodges didn't waste any time going out to the old settlement. I'm sure they'll poke around a lot more over there while they're here. We need to get ahead of this as soon as possible."

"Thank you for the heads up. I'll touch base with her today," Janice said as she hung up once more.

"Let's find out what your plans are, Ms. Jones," Janice mumbled as she grabbed her jacket and walked to the front door.

CHAPTER 4

The sunlight struggled to penetrate the white gossamer like clouds on the early afternoon frigid day. Ms. Jones swore it was colder in her dingy motel room than it was outside in the winter air. She had lived most of her life in New York. It wasn't the cold that made her uncomfortable, but the condition of the town's only motel. It was subpar, in the most generous sense of the word. This wasn't a matter of being some sort of Yankee snob. Ms. Jones's family had few possessions growing up, and she had worked hard to reach the status she held in one of the toughest cities in the country. Ashley Jones was an Ivy League graduate and the equivalent of a great white land shark when it came to real estate. She preferred life's more rewarding things and avoided all things that reminded her of her tough upbringing.

The motel was built the better part of thirty years ago. Its eight-room capacity was as sufficient for today as it was for back then, more so now that the town only had a population of fifty-eight people at the most. Each room contained a bed, a bathroom, and not much else. The walls were covered in ripped, faded, and molded wallpaper, along with stained furniture, as an unfortunate accent that looked more like soak-stained paintings.

Ms. Jones assumed the motel attracted little business, outside of cheap tourists who stayed at the Dalyville Inn while visiting Nashville and refusing to spend the cash to stay comfortably in the city. Other than that, the town's population hadn't grown since the motel was built, and there wasn't much need for one in the town.

The old man behind the desk in the motel's office mentioned that only those who heard of the original settlement, a couple of crooked paranormal investigators, and a steady supply of visiting college students who wanted an off-the-grid party spot were the extent of outsiders that passed through a town on its deathbed.

The once attractive, luminescent motel's sign was no longer bright and already had several missing letters needed to complete the spelling of Dalyville Inn. The chipped and peeled paint had seen better days. If one wasn't paying attention, it would be easy to assume the place had been abandoned long ago. Ms. Jones kicked at the floor-based radiator, which spewed more of a high-pitch grinding noise than heat, but it was a great distraction from the dreary, yellowish shaded walls and dingy furniture. She was sure Tammy could hear her from the room next to hers and calmed down just a little to maintain her normally stern and in control disposition. Ms. Jones didn't want Tammy coming over and asking questions and she definitely didn't want Tammy to see an out of character emotional response to her frustration with the accommodations. She needed to keep the persona of being a well put together, smart, calm, and savvy woman for all that encountered her, which included her long-time assistant. It was a needed disposition in Ms. Jones' line of work. No sexist, condescending man could ever get this type of emotional reaction from her at a negotiating table. What would it look like to Tammy if she found her going "Foxy Brown" on a radiator that had superb odds of being older than her boss? At this point, a welcome distraction knocked at the door.

"Ms. Jones, are you there?" The female voice on the other side of the door yelled out.

Ms. Jones straightened her clothes and hair and gathered herself after her outburst of anger. A quick inhale and exhale, then she unlocked and opened the door. A beautiful African American woman stood on the other side. Her silky black hair had a few strands of gray that sat perfectly in place and covered one of her almond-shaped brown eyes. The unexpected guest dressed casually, with a blue blouse, denim jeans, and running shoes. Although she was short in stature, her posture was nothing short of perfection. She carried herself in a way that made it clear there was a level of respect she expected to receive from everyone. Ms. Jones liked her already.

"Hello. Yes, I'm Ms. Jones, and you are?" she said, reaching her hand out.

"Hi, I'm Janice Williams. I'm one of the residents of the town. Do you mind if I come in?"

"No, not at all. Come on in." Ms. Jones smiled as she stepped aside.

"Ms. Jones, I know you don't know me, so I'll get straight to the point. I need your cooperation and your discretion in the matter I'm investigating, if you don't mind."

"No," Ms. Jones responded. "I don't know you. So, it will depend on what you have to tell me and whether my cooperation and discretion are warranted. You're the only other person with my skin complexation I've seen in this godforsaken town, and you seem friendly enough, so I would hope you aren't here to deter me from my plans for this land. I've encountered enough resistance ever since my investor group set foot here."

"I'm not here to deter you. I'm here to warn you and maybe get a bit of an idea of what you have planned here. As I've already said, my name is Janice Williams, Former Special Agent Janice Williams of the FBI. Do you mind if I take you to lunch? We have a lot to talk about."

"FBI? What interest would the FBI have in my real estate development project?" Ms. Jones inquired; her brow furrowed in confusion.

"I would be happy to answer any of your questions over lunch. It's important that you see the faces of the townsfolk yourself while we discuss this. You'll get a better feel for what I'm saying if you see for yourself." Janice pulled her credentials from her pocket and showed them to her.

"Okay. Fine. I'll grab my purse."

THE QUICK FIVE-MINUTE drive down Main Street allowed for a fast arrival at Janice's preferred cozy lunch spot. It wasn't just because of the lack of options. Janice was a fan of one of the owners of the place. The building was in better condition than most in the town. Its appearance was clean enough. Although, Janice wouldn't put any money on a bet that it would pass a health inspection. There wasn't an inspector in town anyway. The fresh coat of hot pink paint was eye-catching, along with several high-profile signs that bragged on one particular dish.

"This place has the best lunch in town, which isn't saying much. Famous for its pork stew, but I only get the cheeseburgers since I've been living here. The owners are pretty good people as well," Janice said, as she squeezed into the last parking spot in front.

Several pickup trucks already filled most of the parking spots.

"The Dalyville Diner? Do these people have any creativity when it comes to names for their businesses?" Ms. Jones asked in a snarky tone.

"Not particularly." Janice chuckled.

"Home of the world-famous pork stew," Ms. Jones read the sign mounted in the front window. "I venture to say that's a bit of an exaggeration. Is it any good?"

"I wouldn't know. My family and I don't eat pork, but the owners used to be pig farmers before all the farms in town went under. I would assume since they have that type of experience with pigs they might have a few recipes up their sleeves," Janice replied.

As both ladies entered the diner, the patrons inside the half-filled restaurant immediately stopped their consumptions and conversations and gawked at them as if they were some sort of circus freak show come to town. There wasn't a smile to be found among them, except for one.

"Hey there, Janice. It's good to see you again, darlin'. Grab a seat, and I'll have Jessie come right over and take your order. How's that handsome boy of yours doin'?" Sissy asked with a welcoming smile on her face. Sissy's chubby cheeks stretched to capacity, and the front of her waitress uniform hugged her plump stomach.

"She has a reputation for her upbeat demeanor. The partner and wife of the owner, Mr. Donald Kelly," Janice whispered into Ms. Jones' ear, as she leaned over slightly. "Good to be back, Sissy. It's good to see you too. Jackson is doing well. Do you have some of those delicious cheeseburgers today?" Janice asked, a smile prominently displayed.

"You know it, darlin'. You and your friend grab yourselves a seat. You still don't want to try our world-famous stew?" Sissy replied.

"Good afternoon, everyone," Janice yelled out, greeting the sparse crowd inside.

The diner again fell silent. No one returned the common courtesy. The icy stares remained as Janice and Ms. Jones sat at the table in the far corner of the diner. The vantage point allowed

Janice to have a clear view of the door and all the patrons, which included one particular couple that sat at the opposite end near the door.

"Hey there, ladies, what can I get for ya' today?" the tall slender blonde woman asked. Her long hair and facial features had a striking resemblance to Sissy. The almond shape of her eyes, silky blonde hair and raised cheekbones met all the markers of the classic European beauty traits.

"Hey there, Jessie. Give us two of those 'Homemade Cheese-burgers', will ya? I would love for Ms. Jones here to get a taste of some of Dalyville's fine southern cuisine," Janice said, as she read the items on the menu. The menus were already taped down to the table and visible from both sides. The four menu options were barely clear enough to read past the dirt and grimy grease stains. Classy.

"Sure thing, sweetie. Would you like two sweet teas with that?" Jessie asked. Two rows of pearly white teeth proudly display with her smile. Her smile was as natural and genuine as Sissy's.

"Of course," Ms. Jones added with her own smile present.

"Comin' right up, ladies."

The two continued to peer around and watch as the other patrons stared at them with what could only be described as contempt. After what felt like several minutes to Ms. Jones, the other patrons lowered their eyes and continued to eat their lunch. All except two people. Both glared in their directions with curled lips and squinted eyes, as if they caught the aroma of spoiled garbage leaking from the kitchen.

"Agent Williams, what am I doing here? What do you want?" Ms. Jones asked as her head swayed side to side, observing her surroundings.

"Shhh! Please call me Janice. No one here knows what I used to do for a living. We need to keep our voices down. I didn't expect this much of a crowd in here this late in the afternoon, but I knew two particular people would be here," She nodded in the snarling couple's direction. "I know why you're here, Ms. Jones. What you're doing is ambitious and admirable. I get it. I really do. This town can use the financial influx, but what are your plans for the original settlement site?" Janice asked as she slightly bit her bottom lip and peeled away at her fingernails.

"I'm not sure of what it will be yet. Complete demolishing or renovation, but most likely, it will be the site of the City Hall. I just saw it for the first time yesterday. My project manager didn't do it justice. It's a beautiful piece of land."

"Do you know anything about its history?" Janice inserted.

"No. Just that it's the original Dalyville settlement. Janice, why—"

"Here ya go, darlins." Two plated homemade cheeseburgers filled with toppings and fries were sat down in front of them. "Be careful now 'cause they're really hot. And two ice cold southern sweet teas to wash it all down with. Enjoy!" Jessie interrupted as she placed the meals on the table and scurried off to other nearby patrons. Her smile was just as bright and cheerful as she approached each patron.

"Look, Ms. Jones, what I'm about to tell you will be a little hard to deal with. It will be unsettling, but also confidential. I think it's necessary because I don't know what you might unleash. Whatever is going on, I believe it's contained in that settlement."

"What is it?" Ms. Jones asked, lips curled as she observed the creepy behavior of the strange couple inside the diner, until something else caught her attention.

In the far corner near the entrance, a sepia-colored framed picture of a family hung on the wall near the door. In the picture was an older bearded man with a wide-brimmed hat and what appeared to be a silver haired old lady that could have been the old man's wife. Beside them were two well-dressed kids.

"It's a post-mortem picture. Descendants of the Dalys. Creepy, isn't it? Do you see that couple over there? The ones that have been giving us looks filled with bad intentions since we stepped foot through the door?" Janice asked.

"Yes, I've noticed them. They don't seem to like us very much," Ms. Jones answered.

"That's because they don't. As a whole, this town doesn't like outsiders. I've been living here for fifteen years, and I have exactly one friend here. Few of them care for the color of our skin either, but that's Jarrius and Jean Daly. Most of the town calls him Jerry. They absolutely abhor outsiders and are racist and vile human beings. They don't try to hide it either. Jerry also happens to be the descendant of one of the original Irish settlers of this town. Back when it was going to be called the Town of Gallagher. He's also the mayor," Janice whispered.

Ms. Jones glanced over at the still snarling couple. Jean leaned over closer to Jerry and whispered something to her husband. Janice couldn't quite make out what she said.

"I'm familiar with the name. They were the family that refused to sell their property to any of the investors, no matter the price. As a matter of fact, it was the largest plot of land here outside of the settlement," Ms. Jones whispered as she turned and looked over her shoulder at the Dalys at the counter. "Well, Janice, you are right about one thing. They look like pretty nasty human beings to me." Ms. Jones said, her stare lingered in the Dalys direction.

"Calling them human beings is a bit of a stretch. Ignorance runs in their blood. The Gallaghers and Dalys came over here from Ireland sometime in the early 1800s with about seven other families. It was the Gallaghers and Dalys who led the migration, but the families didn't always see eye to eye. Most of the families were poor, except for the Gallaghers and Dalys. The Gallaghers were the wealthiest, which wasn't saying much compared to other families that traveled with them. They were the only family to own a slave, a young woman by the name of Hannah."

"Of course they did," Ms. Jones replied. "By the looks of them, I'm sure they would like to have one right now."

"Yeah, I'm sure. Listen, you need to know this. They were all farmers, but the Dalys wanted to settle closer to the river. Easier to get drinking water, and water for farming. The Gallaghers wanted what eventually became the original settlement. They wanted to be away from the river in case of flooding. The Gallaghers wanted to build wells and use the groundwater produced from the river. Eventually, the debate became heated, and the two families had a fallout. The Gallaghers won. The argument was heated, and the men of both families settled it with their fist."

The thunderous rumblings of chairs pushing across the floor interrupted Janice as she filled in Ms. Jones on the details. Jerry and Jean stood to their feet and tossed money onto the table.

"Hey, Sissy, it's too dark in here. Ruined our appetite. We'll be back when it lightens up a little, and do something about the smell, will ya?" Jerry spewed as spit flew from his mouth, and his eyes intentionally fixed in Janice and Ms. Jones's direction.

"Jerry Daly! You hush your mouth and leave my place. Everybody is welcome here at the Dalyville Diner," Sissy rebutted.

The Dalys stormed out of the diner, their angry glares still pointed in Janice and Ms. Jones's direction.

"Family blood feud. Literally, a tale as old as time. What's so special about that story that I needed to hear it from an FBI agent?" Ms. Jones asked.

"Is this place called the Town of Gallagher? It's what happened next that started something… unnatural."

"After building the structures you saw earlier with the sheriff, and the digging and construction of the first well, something happened. Hannah saw an opportunity to get her freedom. One night, she waited until her master and mistress turned in for the night. She snuck into their living quarters and put an axe into both of their skulls, and fled."

"Oh my God!" Ms. Jones yelled, swiftly covered her mouth with her hand, and checked to see who may have heard her. "Don't get me wrong, I understand why she did it, but that's so brutal."

"Unfortunately, she didn't make it very far. Once the town found out what happened the next morning, a mob led by the Dalys hunted her down, beat her, and dragged her back to the settlement. They hung her and dumped her into that well. On top of that, they threw the carcasses of the Gallaghers down there with her to rot. After that, The Dalys moved the settlement to where it sits today, only a few miles down the road and not far from the river."

"That's horrific. Let me guess, those assholes that just stormed out of here feel all of this is their birthright?" Ms. Jones asked.

"Yes, that's exactly right. There's more, but I can't get into everything right now."

"They would do whatever it takes to sabotage this development, wouldn't they?" Ms. Jones asked.

"It's more than that, Ms. Jones. Something much more. Since then, there have been so many incidents of missing persons here, and what little information I get about them always seems to have some link to that settlement. It's reported that people have gone there for the thrill or curiosity and have never been seen or heard from again. Those that have stayed too long say they hear voices speak to them, but I'm not sure if that's bullshit or not."

Ms. Jones stared at Janice and grinned. "Reported?" She asked, raising one eyebrow. A slow chuckle eventually erupted into a deep belly laugh as she stood. The patrons inside once again stared at them both. Sissy stood behind the counter and watched as the unusual behavior unfolded.

"Nothing conclusive. Just reported. I can't believe I sat through this. This is ridiculous. Thank you for lunch Ag—Umm… Janice. I'm not interested in any more story time," Ms. Jones said as she stepped away from the table.

Janice pulled a twenty-dollar bill from her pocket and threw it onto the table. She managed to grab Ms. Jones by her wrist as she tried to step away.

"Please, listen. I don't know what's brewing out there, but please reconsider what you're doing, at least at the original settlement. Once I can figure out what's going on and put a stop to it, you can continue with your plans," Janice pleaded.

Ms. Jones yanked her arm away from Janice and looked at the faces inside the diner as they all stared back at them. Sissy made her way from behind the counter and walked in her and Janice's direction.

"Janice, not only will my plans continue, but my project manager will be here in a day or so to get things moving. Dalyville's original settlement needs further surveying, and not even your ghost stories are going to prevent that. Goodbye. I'll walk back to the motel," Ms. Jones said as she stomped away.

I need to figure this out, and I need to do it fast. I could really use Nola's help with this one. Unfortunately, she isn't an option for me. I'm on my own. Janice thought as she followed Ms. Jones outside. "Ms. Jones, please. I'm begging you to just wait a little while.

Something is brewing here, and I need to stop it before people start dying."

Ms. Jones briefly paused and stared back at Janice. She shook her head slightly, turned back around, and continued to walk away.

CHAPTER 5

Janice squinted her eyes and pinched the bridge of her nose as she tired from spending most of the next day staring at missing persons photos from reports in the surrounding areas. Thoughts of the conversation she shared with Ms. Jones yesterday at the Dalyville Diner rehashed in her head. The more Janice thought, the more questions festered in her mind.

Hell, I can't even determine that any of these individuals actually stepped foot in this godforsaken town. Now I have Ms. Jones here buying up land, Janice thought. I'm not a fool. She's not telling me everything, and I have a suspicion she knows more about this town than she's letting on. No way you picked this town without learning about everything that is happening here.

The noise of keys rattling on the other side of the front door caused Janice to glance up at the clock. She quickly collected the papers spread across the coffee table and stuffed them into a nearby binder. The beaming faces of Darrius and Jackson immediately brightened the dreary atmosphere she sat in as she reviewed the missing cases. Their boisterous laughter as they wandered through the front door sliced through the weightier vibe Janice fostered when she worked.

"Hey, baby," Darrius said. A wink and a smile followed.

"Hey, boys. What are you two laughing about?" Janice asked.

After standing up from the couch, she rushed over to Jackson and kissed him on the cheek. Janice stared Darrius in the eyes and planted a slow kiss on his lips, stood on her tippy toes, and wrapped her arms around his shoulders before Darrius could answer her question.

"Daddy was giving me a hard time about Kendall today. She brought me some cookies that she and her mama baked last night," Jackson said, looking away from Janice.

"Aww… Jackson's got a girlfriend. Jackson's got a girlfriend!"

"Mama!"

Janice and Darrius chuckled while Jackson tossed his backpack onto the couch, darted to the kitchen, and peered inside the refrigerator.

"We don't have anything to eat in here," Jackson yelled.

"Son, just grab some chips for now. I'm about to start cooking dinner," Darrius said, removing his coat and tie and placing them on the coat rack next to the door. "Honey, I see the binder on the coffee table. Any luck putting the pieces together?"

"Nope. It's frustrating, to say the least. After I met with the investor that came to town, I had quite a few thoughts racing through my head. My gut is telling me she was hiding something. I'm not sure if it's nefarious in nature, but there is more to her story."

"Yeah, I always thought it was weird someone would put so much money into buying up land around here. Have you consulted Nola at all?"

"Darrius, you know damn well we don't talk much anymore. We spoke briefly, but I just couldn't stand to hear her voice once she brought up our parents." Janice sat at the kitchen table and massaged the back of her neck.

Jackson passed her and looked in her direction after he grabbed the chips to vanquish his unyielding teenage boy appetite, his expression saddened, as he continued to the couch.

"Baby, I understand your anger. You've carried this pain for years. You haven't really talked through it, but I can only assume Nola has been carrying the same pain and guilt as well," Darrius said as he walked over to Janice. "You can't keep carrying that anger from the loss. You have to process it. Maybe it's time… maybe it's time for some forgiveness and you two can get through it together. Maybe even hunt down the creature that took your parents from you?"

Janice glared at Darrius with skepticism and halted her self-massage as she contemplated his words.

"Mama," Jackson interjected. "Dad and I were talking in the car on the way home. What if we moved back to New Orleans? I miss Auntie Nola, and I really hate it here."

The noise from the kitchen caused by Darrius shifting of pots fell silent after Jackson's words to his mother. Janice shot her gaze toward Jackson with her brow raised. She glared at Darrius again as he leaned on the counter next to him.

"Is this what you want?" Janice asked.

"I've thought about it. I think it would be good for all of us." Darrius stood and walked closer to her. "Janice, there's nothing for us here. You're retired from the bureau. This town is dead, and your relationship with your sister is broken. I can easily transfer down to New Orleans with the firm. It's a win for all of us."

"Yeah, mama. I would love to go to school down there. Maybe run track. Just think about it. You and Auntie Nola training me to deal with what's out there. I'd be a complete badass."

"Jackson! Watch your language, son."

"Sorry, Dad," Jackson said sheepishly, lowering his head. He cut his eyes back at his mother and smirked.

"Guys, I can see you both feel strongly about this. I'm open to it, but I have to figure out what's happening here, first. It's not a coincidence that this place was almost always mentioned after those people went missing. I have to finish this," Janice answered.

Her eyes filled with tears as she stared at Darrius. He smiled and wrapped his arms around Janice when the sound of the doorbell stopped him in his tracks. Janice, Darrius, and Jackson all stared at each other in disbelief at the intrusive and unexpected sound.

"Were you guys expecting someone?" Janice walked to the door timidly, gazed through the peephole, which revealed nothing but blinding sunlight on the other side of the door.

Janice opened the door. The cold air brushed against her face as she surveyed the porch. A thick brown file bound by a rubber band, with a folded piece of paper on top, lay at the seal of the door frame. Janice took a step back from the doorway, reached down, and grabbed the thick rubber handle from the holster strapped to her lower leg. The silver blade, wide, curved, and pointed at the tip, was tucked back and pressed against her forearm with her hand. Janice stepped onto the porch and found no one in sight.

"Mama, who is it?"

"No one, baby, but it was some sort of delivery." Janice re-holstered the knife and picked up the file.

The sound of the door slamming shut behind her echoed slightly as she rushed back to the sofa and set the file on the coffee table.

Darrius rushed over to Janice and nodded at the folded paper on top of the file. "What does it say?"

Janice's hands shook as she unfolded the paper and read. *I enjoyed our lunch. You knew there was more, I could tell. I'm trusting you with this information.*

Janice spread the contents of the file across the coffee table, while Darrius and Jackson stood on each side of her. Janice's heart pounded as she scanned the papers in front of her. A smile crept upon her face.

"Unbelievable! Now it makes sense," Janice exclaimed.

"What? What makes sense?" Darrius asked.

Janice quickly gathered the papers back into the file and bound it together, leaving it on the coffee table. She made her way to the coat rack and sprinted toward the door.

"Baby, I have to find Ms. Jones and talk to her. I'll be back soon. Get dinner ready. Make sure Jackson gets his homework done and gets his training in as well."

"Janice, what's going on?"

Janice slammed the front door behind her and hurried to her car. She slipped inside and drove into the darkness of the cold night.

CHAPTER 6

Sometimes Janice would be a little too intense for Jackson when it came to his training regimen. On the surface, it was understandable. Training your son to deal with some of the most unspeakable things that stalk the night would apply a significant amount of pressure to any seasoned hunter. At least Darrius assumed it would. It's Jackson. The thought of his child in any sort of danger was terrifying. When Darrius taught him to ride a bike for the first time, he perspired in fear and felt a jolt of pain in his stomach at the sight of every fall. As luck would have it, since Janice was assigned here by the bureau, it's been relatively quiet. Outside of the ongoing investigation of the missing people, Darrius had not felt that type of anxiety for quite a while. Janice or Jackson in imminent danger had not been something that worried him. The bureau dispatched Janice to a few regional incidents over the past fifteen years and she handled them soundly and without issues.

"Homework taken care of?" Darrius asked Jackson after emerging from his bedroom after about an hour or so.

"No sweat, old man." Jackson replied, a smirk slowly crept on his face as he chuckled.

Darrius returned the smile and laughed along with him. "And yet, you still can't whip me in nothing. Not basketball. Not hand to hand. Not even soda pong," Darrius said, continuing to smile.

"Yeah. Yeah, whatever. Is mama back yet? Might as well get this training done."

"She's not back yet. The way your mother slipped away; she probably won't be back for a little while. How about we knock out this training before she gets back," Darrius said. His voice shifted to an uncompromising tone as he walked to the small table near the front door. Jackson's smile fell from his face as he sighed.

"Sure, I guess. Dad, we've done this all week. Can't we take a little break? I'll read a book or something. I just want some rest." Jackson pleaded. He lowered his head and yawned, holding his hand over his mouth.

Darrius retrieved the packaged item from the table and walked back toward his son. Jackson's brow curled with confusion as he glared back at Darrius with his head slightly tilted. Darrius did his best to mimic his own father's look of disappointment because of its effectiveness on him in his younger days, anything to keep Jackson guessing.

"Son, training your mind and body are the most important things in your life right now. There is no time to rest. There is no time for games. Do you understand?" Darrius continued with a furrowed brow and a stern look of disappointment. Jackson looked away; his head still lowered.

A large bright smile grew on Darrius' face and his eyes shined with excitement and a small chuckle poured from him. "OR..." he shouted. Jackson's head lifted quickly. "We can watch the greatest cinematic movie in history!" Darrius yelled, his voice raised a couple of octaves. He held up a DVD, a young black man on the cover in a kung fu pose. The movie had to be at least twenty years old.

"I've been waiting to get this movie in this house for quite a while. I ordered the DVD two weeks ago, and it finally showed up today. Jackson, you're going to love this," Darrius continued as he ran over to the DVD player and popped opened the cardboard packaging and plastic wrapping with his powerful hands.

"Wait, are you serious, dad? But, what about what mama said?" Jackson asked. His bright smile fixed upon his face.

"You don't worry about her. I'll take care of your mother. What we're about to watch should be a young man's rite of passage. Way more important than any hunting duties," Darrius said, as he slid the DVD into the player and powered on the television.

"Well, what's it about?" Jackson asked. "I've never heard of it."

"You never what?" Darrius asked, as he looked at his son with widened eyes. "This movie has everything, kung fu, love, music, and a beautiful woman. This guy's skin even glows when he believes he is 'The Master', Darrius said, holding two fingers up on each hand for quotes. "You're gonna love it! Go pop some popcorn and make sure it's the butter flavored. I hate the kettle stuff."

Jackson hurriedly tossed a couple of bags of popcorn into the microwave as the DVD played the previews of movies released over twenty years ago. Darrius could see his son's slumping shoulders and his smile still lingered on his face. His idea was going according to plan. Get his son to relax and take some pressure off the kid. The bonus of spending some quality time with Jackson made his idea a little sweeter.

Darrius and Jackson sat down on the couch and shoved their hands into the steaming hot bags of popcorn. The enticing aroma of butter-flavored popcorn filled the living room. The opening credits of the movie started, and the weird techno 80s music played as some Kung Fu master chopped flying arrows in half aimed at him.

"Son, your mother and I are hard on you because we know what you might have to face out there. We love you and whether or not you want to be a hunter, we just want you prepared for anything." Darrius said.

"I get it, dad. Mama tells me the same thing all the time."

Darrius smiled as he stared at his son. The techno music from the movie seemed to fade far into the background as he admired the maturity of Jackson. It was these moments Darrius learned to savor. He knew they would become fewer as Jackson grew older.

"Well, remember, as far as your mother is concerned, we had a good day of training. Your mother works you hard enough. Time for some R and R."

"I know the drill, dad. We could use a little break, right? What do you say we crack open a couple of beers and really have a good time?" Jackson asked with another sly grin on his face.

"Don't push it, son," Darrius said as he returned a smile with a quick wink of his eye. "Oh, look. Here comes the scene in the movie theater. This is hilarious."

CHAPTER 7

I sat in the plushy imitation leather chair behind the cheap do-it-yourself particleboard desk, my feet elevated and rested on its edge, my Army boots prominently displayed and untied. The frequent choice of tactical footwear had left subtle scratches on the right edge of my desk. The various papers scattered about its surface were accompanied by the large bottle of vodka and a wide rim glass, along with a large brown envelope and laptop opened to an informational database webpage, 'The History of The Occult and The Macabre'.

I tilted my head back, eyes blurred from my slight intoxication, and ogled the varied police commendations and awards from an assortment of organizations, including the city of New Orleans. Most, given for bravery and leadership, were all conspicuously displayed upon the wall. Two framed and mounted front-page newspapers stood out among the commendations. The sight of the headlines triggered a flood of memories as my hands trembled: 'Lone New Orleans Police

Detective Takes Down Goliath.' The other: 'Police Detective's Parents Slain in Apparent Beast Attack.' The latter headline was only three years old.

Although Janice and I weren't on the best of terms these days, I was still apprehensive about using the internet as a means to gather information on anything supernatural. There were too many hacks with a computer and a website that tossed out misinformation on the internet. I practically felt her judgmental eyes staring at me and heard Janice's voice in my head. Still, there was way too much information on the web to not use it as a source.

The world wide web can't help you with the otherworldly, Nola. It's those musty old books that will get you in position to defeat those monsters.

It didn't matter. I read over the information found on the webpage in front of me, along with many others before it. If the dark web could help me understand exactly what type of lycanthrope attacked and killed my parents, then modern technology was acceptable.

Whatever could help me find that son of a bitch and put it down for good, I thought.

The tip of the bottle kissed the brim of the glass once again as I poured another drink.

"God, I have to quit drinking. How could I have not been there for them? Why does Janice hate me so much? I would never blame her..." I mumbled as I took another sip.

Tears flooded my eyes, and I hurled the glass against the nearby wall. Shards flew as the glass shattered and moistened the wall with vodka.

The faint sound of a gentle knock at the door from a few feet away pulled me from that horrid memory. After those drinks, the faint sound from the door might as well have been the horn of a tugboat floating down the Mississippi River. I tilted my head back in frustration as the knocking continued.

"I'm coming!" I yelled. "Hold your fucking horses." I marched toward the tinted glass-paned door and yanked it open.

The familiar face of a middle-aged, blonde-haired woman, that stood on the other side of the door, stared back at me with a look of disappointment. Her gaudy choice of jewelry was a clear indicator of her old money and privileged status in the city.

"Come in, Mrs. Winslet." The chinchilla shawl wrapped around her shoulders only irritated me at the sight of her. I retreated to the comfortable seat behind the desk.

Even in the winter months, New Orleans didn't get cold enough for a damn chinchilla fur winter wear. The oversized desk between me and whomever sat across from me provided a sense of comfort that mirrored my desire not to get too emotionally involved with anyone outside of family, or just to keep a tactical distance needed from the unpleasant or unexpected person or thing on the other side. Today, it happened to be a client and the stench of her perfume.

"Mrs. Winslet, although it's November, it's still seventy degrees outside. Is it really necessary to tote the fur of dead animals around your shoulders?” I leaned back in my chair and placed my boots back on top of the desk.

“Ms. Maor, it’s ten o’clock in the morning. Is it necessary to reek of alcohol so early?” Her voice was deeper than most men I knew. “Have you made any progress on my case? It’s been four weeks, and I haven’t seen many results, considering the substantial deposit I paid you.”

“I’ve told you before to call me Nola. The formality is only needed on my part. You’re the paying client. Also, if you’d seen half of the shit I’ve had to deal with, you’d drink as well. Actually, there’s been some progress, so I suppose it’s good you came by.”

I picked up the nearby brown envelope on the desk. A look of concern sat upon Mrs. Winslet’s face, as her brow curled and her lips folded inward. Mrs. Winslet leaned in closer to the desk and sat on the edge of the chair to get a better look at the envelope.

“I’ve heard of your fairytales. It’s why I chose you. What have you found?” Mrs. Winslet asked. She rushed over her words and removed the shawl from her shoulders.

I opened the envelope and pulled several photographs from inside, then presented them to her. With the anticipation of the emotional evisceration Mrs. Winslet was about to take, I pulled another glass from the drawer of my desk, poured once again, and took another swallow as she glanced at the photos.

She shuffled through the photographs and slowed down at the last few as her sight lingered on each one. Her eyes welled with tears, and her face became as bright as the Georgia red clay.

"Mrs. Winslet, I hate doing this type of work because it usually results in heartbreak for someone like yourself, but I have to pay the bills. Your husband has opened several offshore accounts and has been funneling money slowly into them in increments of various amounts. Apparently, your wealth is deep enough that he knew you wouldn't notice." I took another swallow. "If my contacts are right, he's stolen approximately four and a half million dollars over a five-year span. Also, I'm gonna assume that young lady in the photo that he's kissing isn't the product of an open relationship between the two of you. I think you may want to secure a talented attorney."

Mrs. Winslet sobbed into her hands as the photos hit the floor. The sound of her cries caused me to shift uncomfortably in the chair and finish the last bit of libation in the glass. She did not strike me as the type of woman that would cry so openly. I suppose the tough outer demeanor was mostly for show.

The cell phone next to my laptop vibrated violently against the desk. The screen illuminated as the words 'Unknown Caller' displayed across it before it fell silent again.

"Mrs. Winslet, I need you to get yourself together and put away the weakness. You need to get a lawyer and get law enforcement involved if needed. Otherwise, your husband will siphon more of your family's money and possibly leave the country with the young lady in the picture."

My tone was emotionless, unable to drum up any empathy inside. My dad and sister always preached about being strong. Somewhere along the way, after the death of my parents, that strength had eventually turned into more of a necessity to close myself off from others.

"The young lady's name is Rebecca Marlow. She's our neighbor's twenty-seven-year-old daughter. You know, you're an incredibly cold asshole, Nola. You just handed me a lifetime of pain and regret, and your words to me were to put away the weakness? I'm a lady, unlike yourself, so I say this with trepidation… fuck you!" Mrs. Winslet fired back. "You could stand to get yourself together as well. You're obviously an alcoholic. I remember Goliath, and if the other tales about you are true, then thank you for doing God's work and putting those monsters down, but you're carrying a tremendous amount of pain. I see the framed headlines behind you."

I stood, ready to unload a barrage of insults in Mrs. Winslet's direction, when my cell phone vibrated again and rattled against the desk.

"Look, what you need to do is mind your own damn business. Pay me the rest of my money and get the hell out of my office."

The glow of the cellphone went dark, only to light again with the words 'two missed calls' displayed on the screen.

Mrs. Winslet glanced down at her own cellphone and keyed in a few strokes. "Thank you for your work, detective. I wired the money to you. I can see what life has done to you, and I can also see how resilient you are. Just don't lose yourself in the pain. Life will eat you alive; just look at me," she said with a slight smirk on her face.

The violent rattle continued. My cellphone seemed louder as my hands shook with another call. "Goodbye, Mrs. Winslet," I yelled as I picked up the phone.

Mrs. Winslet slammed the door behind her.

"Hello," I yelled, answering the call.

"A-Auntie, Nola? This is Jackson," the shaky, timid voice stammered on the other end.

"What do you need, Jackson? I'm busy at the moment."

"I-It's my mom, Auntie. She's… She's dead. Your sister is dead, Auntie Nola."

My hands weakened, and the cellphone dropped to the floor, violently breaking into pieces. My heart sank into my stomach…broken like the dead phone that lay before me.

CHAPTER 8

In some weird way, there was always something I enjoyed about the pressure of an airplane cabin. It had a relaxing effect on me. The leg room left a lot to be desired, but the muzzled sound of the surrounding voices struggled to be heard over both the pressurized environment, and the roar of the engines. It usually allowed me to have a little peace and left me to my own thoughts. Not this time. This time, my head was bombarded with images of Janice and me playing in our front yard as kids. Our training sessions after dealing with Goliath and the Sunday dinners with Mom and Dad were some of the more enjoyable memories of the Maors that provided me comfort in my darkest times.

For now, I have the comfort of this extra-large cup I picked up from a fast-food joint. I filled it with a self-invented blend of vodka and flavored soda from the bars after passing through airport security. I added the additional tiny bottle of rum provided by the flight attendant and turned the little tan colored air conditioning nozzle above my head wide open, allowing the cool air to flow against the scar on my face. I leaned back and rested my head on the seat. The fruity smell of the blended fruit punch and alcohol that permeated from my cup was enticing enough to have one sip after another from a straw.

The sound of my father's voice in my head pushed me to lay off drinking so much so fast. Right behind him, I could hear my mother yell at my dad and tell him to leave me the hell alone. Those interactions with my parents always put them in a different light. The strict Catholic upbringing by my parents had a different effect after I had to deal with that vicious and bloodthirsty monster, Goliath. The faith instilled in me was shaken completely before my encounter with that beast, but with my eyes open to such evils, it somehow resurrected my once dead faith out of me once again. I had the feeling my parents were proud of me and trusted me once again.

It wasn't all sunshine and roses once Mom and Dad found out what Janice and I did for a living. Knowing about the unnatural freaks like Goliath that were out there crippled their reality for a while. It somehow made their faith in God stronger and viewed Janice and me as soldiers of the Lord. No pressure. If I would have paid more attention to things after the minor victory I had as a hunter a day or two before their murder, then maybe everything would be different.

THE KEY *to the deadbolt on the front door I carried since a high school still worked, and I still smiled like a kid given my first taste of adult-*

hood every time I turned it. It made me feel as though those walls would always be home and provided a small sense of stability. Those locks hadn't changed in thirty years.

"Hello, sweetheart. What brings you by today?" Daddy kissed me on the cheek when I walked through the front door.

"Nothing, really, Daddy. I missed you guys, so I decided to stop by." I hugged him tightly. "Where's Mommy?"

"She's upstairs in the office. I'm sure once she hears your voice, she'll be running down any moment."

I looked at my father and noticed he wore the brown knitted sweater I bought him for Father's Day almost six years ago. Its V-shaped collar went all the way down to three large brown buttons that were fastened but were most likely being tested to their maximum capacity by the extra weight in his belly.

"Daddy, Janice and I got this sweater for you over six years ago. I'm not sure it quite fits the same anymore." I giggled a little at the perplexed look on his face.

"I love my sweater, and it fits just fine." He scratched his beard as he spoke in his raspy voice. "Besides, I want to hear about some monster's ass you've kicked lately." He said as he mimicked a boxer punching at the air.

The sound of the creaking stairs beside me was accompanied by the thumps of the rapidly descending footsteps. I turned to investigate the sound and watched my beautiful mother smiling back at me. Her hair was pulled back in a ponytail; as it swayed back and forth with her energetic, bouncing walk down the staircase.

"Edward, would you please leave Nola alone? I'm sure she doesn't want to talk shop if she took the time out to see her precious mother," my mother said.

"You mean her precious parents, don't you, Ruth?" my father retorted.

"Oh, you hush, old man," my mother replied.

"Mama, what is that smell? It smells like pure heaven in here, and by heaven, I mean blueberry muffins. Are you baking blueberry muffins?"

"Of course! I had a feeling you would stop by. You mentioned you missed Daddy and me. That usually means you'll make some time for us out of your busy schedule."

"Mama, I'll be right back. Let me talk with Daddy a bit. I know he's itching to talk to me about what's going on out there."

"Go 'head, baby. I'll be in the kitchen," Ruth replied.

A brief stroll into the living room and my father was already blissfully involved in some sort of 80s action flick as he laid back in his time worn recliner. The recliner had seen better days. Once a clean, smooth, chocolate-colored, covered fabric, it was now torn in various places and painted with the stains of devoured snacks of the past. I found it disgusting, but any suggestions of replacing it would send my father into a lecture that would rival any of the greatest lawyers or debaters in history. He sat in the center of the living room next to the sofa and watched his large screen TV mounted onto the wall. The tangerine hue from the sunset peered through the three windows only slightly covered by my mother's daisy flower patterned curtains. It made for a relaxing and inviting environment that my father took advantage of every chance he could.

"So, Daddy, what have you been up to?"

"Not much, baby. Keeping tabs on the news headlines here and in Tennessee and keeping an eye on you and your sister. Other than that, letting your mother believe she's in charge," he said with a sly grin on his face.

I couldn't help but laugh at his retort. He epitomized the demeanor of a traditional man. He made sure his wife and kids were protected and taken care of, and I'm sure he wouldn't have it any other way. Now, after years of working on offshore refineries, he's earned the right to relax and enjoy his time.

"Nola, baby, have you talked to your sister lately? What's she up to?"

"I have. We talked about how much Jackson is growing up and the missing persons cases she's working on. Other than that, there wasn't much to talk about. Most likely because Janice and I talk so often, sometimes the conversations get a bit stale," I replied.

As I walked over to him, I rubbed the top of his balding head and the smile on his face grew larger. Daddy wasn't shy about showing his love and affection, and he always appreciated it when the gestures were returned.

"That's a shame. All the way to Tennessee for missing persons? Seems like a waste of time. I was watching the news a couple of days ago, and they were talking about a dismembered body. Is that something you're looking into, Nola?"

"Oh, do I have a story for you, Daddy. That body is the victim of some sort of lycanthrope that has been on the loose in the city. It hasn't killed often, but it's different from others that I've put down. I cornered it in an abandoned building, shot it, and hit it at least twice

with a silver bullet. It bled, but the shots didn't kill it. I had to fight it off with a couple of blades and with more rounds from Corbin. Nothing really seemed to slow it down much. It chased me for a bit, but I was able to get away from it. The frickin' thing was huge."

The look of excitement on my father's face waned as I gave him the details. His eyes widened as he stared back at me.

"Nola, this isn't like Goliath, is it?"

"No Daddy. It was definitely a werewolf. I haven't seen them here in New Orleans often. The weird thing about this one was not only the size and its resistance to silver, but it wasn't a full moon, and yet there it stood."

"I usually like your hunting stories. Something feels different about this, and not in a good way. I know you're good at what you do, but I hope you're taking this thing seriously. Don't underestimate it."

The screeching tires of a car speeding off outside the window on the right side of where my father sat interrupted our conversation. It always bothered me how some idiots sped down residential streets and endangered the lives of people, especially children.

"Goddammit! Not that idiot again," my father yelled as he stood from his recliner and made his way to the window.

"What is it, Daddy? Has this happened before?" I followed him to the window.

"Edward, was it that knucklehead again?" My mother ran into the room with a look of worry planted upon her face.

"That asshole has been doing that for more than two days now. Sometimes he just sits there, then peels off and speeds down the street.

Never really got a good look at his face, though, and the police won't even come out about it," Edward said.

A weight of discomfort pulled at my stomach as if someone strapped a weight around me. The sight of the anxiousness displayed by my parents made me uncomfortable.

"Guys, I'm going to hang back tonight and sleep in my old bedroom. Just to be sure everything is okay around here, and to make sure I get plenty of Mama's cooking tonight."

THE TWIN BED I slept in all of my adolescent life wasn't as comfortable as I remembered. It could have been the fact that I was still fully dressed—boots and all. I rested those boots on the footboard of the now too short bed frame. I couldn't believe I had so many drooling induced deep slumbers in this sad sack of a bed. Even if I wasn't on edge about the strange occurrence that happened earlier today outside my parents' window, something told me that I still wouldn't get much sleep.

The not-so-subtle sound of the floorboard as it creaked outside of my childhood bedroom caught my attention. It was well known in my house that the familiar sounds of the creaking floorboards served as a makeshift alarm for teenage daughters trying to sneak in or out of the house in the middle of the night. The only issue was there were no teenage daughters in the house, and there was no reason for anyone to be in the hallway. Although, my father was known to sneak out of the bed in the middle of the night to watch TV in the living room during his episodes of insomnia.

It's probably nothing. I'll just check to be sure. Knowing Daddy, he probably has a lot on his mind, I thought as I climbed out of the noisy, uncomfortable twin bed.

I grabbed Corbin from the nightstand and timidly crept out of my old bedroom to investigate the hallway. The newly purchased revolver was still taking some getting used to. Its weight always felt a little heavy on the front end, but I had never shot more accurately with another handgun. It was the intimidating grid pattern on its onyx plating that made it so attractive to me. The stopping power and the ability to knock the biggest manner of beast on its ass didn't hurt, either.

The deafening silence of the open hallway blanketed the air, caused the tiny hairs on my neck to stand. If Daddy was downstairs watching TV, I would be able to hear it from up here, or at least near the staircase. The inside of my nostrils stung at the unexpected stench of the earthy odor of a wet dog in the hallway. A low rumble of noise that sounded much like a subtle growl came from my parents' bedroom. It was unfamiliar and far from the sound of my father's snoring I had become accustomed to during my earlier years.

I continued down the hallway and slowly crept toward my parents' door. The silence on the other side of the door was unsettling as I pressed my ear against the cool door of the bedroom. The growl I thought I heard was no longer present. After a few brief moments, the door vibrated with the sound of heavy breathing on the other side. The leaden reverberation of scratching followed as it started a couple of feet above my head and made its way down. That sound on the other side of the door made its way down to my head and triangular shaped razor-sharp claws penetrated the wooden door and sliced through it like paper. The thunderous roar on the other side sent vibrations through the door and down my spine. Eyes wide, I stumbled backward and pointed Corbin toward the unusually enormous claws.

A second set of claws penetrated through the wood and splintered the door to pieces. The sooty colored creature that emerged squatted as it walked out of my parents' bedroom. Its powerful bristly hair covered body broke away pieces of the door frame as it came through. It bared its oversized canine teeth at me, covered in blood.

Again, I raised Corbin and pointed. My aim was shaky as my hands violently trembled. The barrel of the revolver jumped as I fired several shots of silver rounds into the werewolf's chest. It roared in pain. The sound reverberated in my chest as I watched its massive claws grab at its wounds. I exhaled sharply and leaned against the balcony banister in relief. The beast stumbled back against the wall that crumbled and folded inward as if it was paper.

Werewolves were mean and nasty creatures. This one was the biggest I had ever seen. Whatever the size, silver would always put one down for good. My eyes widened at the sight of what had happened next. The beast stood on its clawed feet again, and its body spit the rounds from its chest. It extended its arms and released a ferocious roar, baring its sharp teeth at me once again. I looked past it and saw the bloodied bodies of my parents lying in bed.

"No! What have you done?" I screamed at it, while tears fell from my eyes.

The sizable beast moved swiftly as it closed the space between us and wrapped its massive claws around my throat. It lifted me in the air with little effort, taking the sharp claw of one finger and slicing me deeply across my cheek. The would-be searing pain of the cut dulled by the elevated sight of my mutilated parents in the other room. The *fiery red glow of its eyes was the last thing I saw of the beast as it threw me over the second-floor banister, and I fell to the living room floor below...*

THE DING of the *fasten seatbelt* sign shook me from my deep reflection of that night. I clutched the armrest of the bolted down airplane chair. My hands shook and sharp pains assaulted my stomach. Several deep breaths calmed me as the airplane's intercom system prompted and chimed.

"As we start our descent, it's a frigid twenty-eight degrees with clear skies in Nashville, Tennessee. Just for your information, there is a cold front headed this way that will plunge those temperatures even further. Hope you brought a sweater. Please put all tray tables and chairs in their upright positions and fasten your seatbelts. We should be landing shortly. Enjoy your time in Nashville, and thank you for flying with us." The pilot's cheerful voice was gone as fast as it made its presence.

As my anxiety calmed, I rubbed the deep scar on my cheek that seemed to be the primary source of entertainment for the flight attendant every time she passed by and gawked. I shifted in my seat, eager for the plane to land and anxious to get off. My mind was consumed with one thought.

I can't let down any more family.

CHAPTER 9

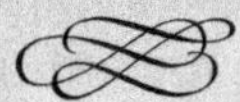

The overly cautious cabdriver drove well below the posted speed limits from Nashville's airport. As I stared out the window at the acres of woodland, the timid nature of the ride irritated me. The forest wasn't a sight I was used to, at least not at the thickness of what was ahead. Even a small city as unique as New Orleans, it was still a city, covered in concrete and steel. Although the urgency of the driver left a lot to be desired, it allowed me time to admire the all-consuming nature of the tree line that sandwiched the narrow road he drove. The forest was beautiful and absolute in its nature; it appeared to be unforgiving if someone ignorant to its nature ventured off into it.

I couldn't believe I picked the one cabdriver that preferred to drive without any music or engage in conversation. With my recent run of luck lately, that was a little good fortune. Still, the smell of stale cigarettes nauseated me, and only added to the sharp throbbing pain in my stomach. The rhythmic hum of the tires as they pushed against the road had a calming effect. I needed it since I spent the entire ride inside my head a lot longer than I preferred, especially sober. Reflecting on the wilted relationship between my sister and me, I could only wonder what I could have done differently. A change in tone could have made all the difference when we spoke to each other. Instead, the last conversation Janice and I had now haunted my mind and filled me with regret.

Fifteen years and I didn't take one trip out here to visit. She always came home. She always came to me, I thought as my leg shook uncontrollably and tears fell down my face.

Both Janice and I had the propensity to use our jobs as an excuse not to visit the other. My world opened up after Goliath. There was always some bogeyman or supernatural threat that needed to be hunted down and destroyed, which took priority, especially after the death of Mom and Dad. Besides, Janice always came to New Orleans with the boys to visit before. She always told me there was no reason to come to Dalyville. There was nothing out there to see. By the look of things, she wasn't wrong. I glanced up at the driver and shook my head in disbelief as he stared out the windshield, stiff and motionless. It was as if the car was automated or driven by some sort of life like robot. At a minimum, he shared the personality of one.

"Ma'am, are you okay?" the cab driver asked as he broke his silence.

"Fine."

"I only ask because you're shaking a lot and crying," he continued.

"I said I'm fine. Just colder than I expected, that's all."

I quickly wiped the tears away and took a deep breath. An emotional breakdown in front of some stranger wasn't an option.

"You know, I almost put you out when you told me where you were going," the cabdriver said. His overgrown mustache was thick enough I couldn't see his lips move when he spoke.

"Excuse me. You almost did what?"

"This town isn't right. There are some nice people that live there, but mostly that town isn't right. It has an ugly side to it."

"Well, it doesn't matter much what's there or what the people are like. I need to go there."

He stared back at me through the rearview mirror as if he wanted my undivided attention. "Miss, I don't know you, but you need to open your ears to what I'm trying to tell ya. These people don't like outsiders. The entire town is creepy, unnatural, even."

"Sir, I just told you, I need to go there. My sister died, and I need to see my family. It doesn't matter what's going on there."

"You kin to the black lady that lives there? Is that your sister?"

I looked back at him through the rearview mirror. His eyes moved only briefly to maintain safety on the road.

"Who the hell are you?" My brow furrowed as my eyes locked with his.

"I used to live there. All of my life, actually. That is, until last year. Your sister and her family were the only black people living there. My family's descendants were one of the seven founding families of this town. I'm the last surviving member of my family. Once my parents died, I got the hell out of there."

My curiosity had gotten the best of me. "Why did you leave if your family has such a history there?"

"My parents used to tell me about the nasty ways of the Dalys back in the beginning of everything. Told me they were some hateful and power-hungry people. I can't say much has changed over the generations."

"So, you left your home because of a family you didn't like? It doesn't sound like you have any balls at all," I said. I averted my eyes after I listened to the rudeness that spewed from me. A display of anger and frustration that momentarily slipped away. "I apologize. I didn't mean to—"

"Don't mention it. I need ya to listen to me. The Dalys weren't entirely the reason I left. All the other descendants of the founding families are dead. That's bad enough, but now people have gone missing," he continued.

"I've heard some things about that. How could you be so sure?"

"I've seen a couple of them before they went missing." His eyes once again glared back at me through the mirror.

An unusually large yellow and green sign served as a brief distraction, and its wording provided a welcome sigh of relief.

"Welcome to Dalyville, Miss. Population fifty-eight, very unusual people. I'm sorry for your loss. The medical examiner and the mortician are the same person here. Main Street stretches a few miles, with only about six roads that branch off. The town is right up ahead, here. It looks like the sheriff and the mortician are already there. I can see their cars out front. If you don't mind, can you pay me now? I don't want to be there any longer than I have to be. There was a reason I escaped." The driver gawked at me with wide, fearful eyes in the rear-view mirror.

"Um… okay. That's not a problem," I replied.

I shook my head as I dug in my bag for cash, still a bit confused by the sudden chattiness of the cabdriver. After I pulled the sixty bucks from my wallet, I leaned forward to hand it to him and noticed how pale his face had become. His hands shook as he reached back for the cash.

The car engine revved, and the car accelerated as he shifted his eyes repeatedly from the road ahead into the rearview mirror at me. My focus was now solely on the driver, and his erratic behavior, and his visible apprehension of returning to Dalyville.

"I'm sorry, did you say you escaped from Dalyville?" I asked.

"Poor choice of words, I suppose. I just mean I managed to save enough to move away," he replied.

"Ah… I see." My eyes were still affixed on him. "I'm sorry, but you wanted me to pay you now, yet the meter is still running. You said you see the sheriff's car, but I only see trees. So, either you're a terrible cabdriver, or you're an awful liar."

The driver looked back once again as the never-ending treeline ended. The sun was no longer blocked by the imposing height of the trees.

"Ma'am, we're here. Thank you for the fare. Welcome to Dalyville, Tennessee," the cabdriver stated, nodding in the direction of the door handle, insisting on my exit.

I grabbed my bag and exited the cab, then nodded in return. The fear and anxiousness on his face was familiar, something I had seen far too many times before in others. The cab sped off, kicking a significant amount of dust into the air before I could close the rear door. I turned and read the name on the building with the police vehicle parked in front.

"Nicholson's Mortuary," I mumbled, with a heavy sigh that followed. The sound of the name as it passed my lips was like a punch to the gut, reminding me of the reason I was in this shitty little town in the first place.

The door to the mortuary opened, and a uniformed law enforcement officer stepped outside. He squinted his eyes at the brightness of the sunshine as he tilted the acorn-colored, over-sized, round brim hat on his head. The kind so often worn by highway patrolmen. The hat was the same color as his fitted uniform. The sheriff's confident stride down the few stairs in front of the mortuary reminded me of those cheesy overly macho action stars of the 90s. His thick frame fell in line with stereotypical, cornfed country men.

"Howdy, ma'am. You must be Nola Maor?" Sheriff Alfred asked.

"I am. It's a pleasure to meet you, Sheriff. Janice mentioned you quite a few times when we talked. Where is she?" I replied, my singular focus on Janice.

"She's inside. But before we go in, we should talk."

"Sheriff, I have nothing to talk about. What I need is for you to get out of my way so I can see my sister. If you don't move, it won't be pretty for you."

A quick pace up the few stairs in front put me nose to nose with the sheriff.

Sheriff Alfred grinned at me, standing his ground and displaying his lack of fear. After a few brief moments, he took a couple of steps backward, his eyebrows raised, and his sly grin still apparent behind his beard.

"Hold on a second, Ms. Maor. I'm not your enemy. Your sister and I were pretty open friends. I knew all about her assignments and what she did for a living. Janice even told me a lot about you. She forgot to mention you were five-foot-nine, with your set of skills. I assume you have the same fighting skills as your sister?" The sheriff paused as he stared at the scar on my face. "Doesn't matter. I still feel like I know you. I'll take you inside, but she doesn't look like herself." His voice trailed off as if it pained him to say it. He held the door open for me to enter.

The floor felt as if disembodied hands reached up and pulled at my legs as I walked down the narrow, ivory-colored, tiled hall-way. Every step was like dredging through waist deep water. My breaths labored and hands trembled and perspired as they pulled at each other. Dread filled me. Thoughts wandered again to days past when Janice and I played in the front yard at home. The thump of the red ball as it bounced against the cardboard sprawled out by my father was clear in my head. The cardboard was there so we didn't sit on the scorching pavement that baked under the New Orleans sun. I watched as Janice flawlessly scooped up one jack after another... ones, sets of twos, threes, and so forth. I could never beat her. Janice's reflexes were always far superior to my own. At some point, I stopped trying to beat her. I just marveled at my big sister's ability to pick up all those jacks, no matter how spread out they were, all in one swoop, red ball included. Janice, to her credit, never stopped trying to teach me.

I expected to visit Janice here in Dalyville one day soon. She knew it would take some time. Old wounds from the past still hadn't healed, but my desire to rekindle the relationship we had so long ago was held back by our own stubbornness and pride. What I never expected was to visit Janice in these conditions.

"It's the set of doors straight ahead, ma'am," Sheriff Alfred said.

Alfred opened the heavy stainless steel plated doors as I eyed the dingy sign mounted above it. Those frequent trips to the morgue as part of the duties of a detective with the New Orleans Police Department, and even as a private investigator, were never what I would consider a desirable part of the job. The distinctive, sickly sweet odor of formaldehyde and various chemicals, blended with the stench of decaying flesh from dead bodies, somehow reminded me of the smell of nail polish remover.

"Dr. Vornado, this is Nola Maor. She's here to identify the body," Sheriff Alfred said.

"Hello, Ms. Maor," Dr. Vornado greeted, as he extended his pale hand. A smile prominently displayed the rows of yellow and black teeth protruding from his overbite. The aged white medical coat was unkept with a collection of wrinkles and a splattering of unknown stains. The large coat swallowed his thin frame. "Oh, I would hate to play cards with you, Ms. Maor. You have a pretty good poker face. I usually creep out most people. I didn't always look like this. I was quite handsome back in my day." He nodded toward a picture of a young man wearing what appeared to be the same white medical coat, which seemed to fit much better.

"Hello, Doctor. I'm not most people, and I'm not interested in your stories. I've come a long way, and I'd like to get this over with," I replied, shaking his thin, frail, icy hands. The doctor's skin was soft and loose. It felt as if it would slide off the bones in his hand if my handshake was too firm.

"Ms. Maor, I must warn you, what you are about to see is very, uh, unsettling. The sheriff spared your brother-in-law the unfortunate task of identifying his wife. It definitely would have been too much for the boy. I've seen nothing like this in my entire career."

Dr. Vornado walked over to the bright white sheet, which covered the human silhouette that rested on the table. His hands trembled as he leaned in to pull back the sheet. A slight hesitation in Dr. Vornado's movement furthered the discomfort in both the sheriff and me as we gave each other an uncomfortable glance.

My body tensed. My heart thumped in my chest as I watched his frail hands grip the fabric. The room felt as if it was draining the life from my body, aching to make me a resident. I widened my eyes at the sight of the sheet removed. I inhaled sharply; my lower jaw trembled as my eyes filled with tears. Legs weakened, I timidly walked closer to the disfigured body and held her stiffened hand just above Janice's shriveled, charcoal-colored skin. Black sludge poured from the empty void where her eyes had once occupied.

"I don't understand. What could have done this? S-she doesn't even look human anymore," I said, with a stiffened face and a monotone voice as tears fell from my eyes.

"Like I said before, Ms. Maor, I've never seen anything like this in my life. The epidermis is completely discolored and dehydrated, along with all the muscle and tissue underneath. The orbital cavities are completely void of the ophthalmologic systems. The thick black liquid you see here has the same consistency as pus, but it has an odor similar to tar."

"My, God," Sheriff Alfred mumbled.

"Ms. Maor, I know your sister was in her early forties, but did she have a complete head of gray hair this early in life?"

"No. Whatever did this turned her hair gray as well. Dr. Vornado, if there hasn't been any other bodies that came through the morgue that look like this, has anybody in town complained of illness?" I wiped the tears from my face.

"None that I'm aware of," Dr. Vornado replied.

"Are you aware of any chemicals or poisons that can do this much damage in such a short time frame?"

"Nothing I'm aware of, Ms. Maor. I'm the only examiner here. We're a town of only fifty or so people. In fact, we aren't much of a town at all. I'm sorry for your loss. Do you have any instructions on the care of the remains?"

I pulled my eyes away from Janice and glanced over at the doctor, then at the sheriff. The pain inside me quickly morphed into a rage that I tried not to show. My brow furrowed as I exhaled deeply again and gazed upon Janice one last time.

"Ship her to New Orleans. I'll forward you the address of the mortuary. I want my sister buried at home. Sheriff, I need to speak to you alone, and I need a ride to my sister's home," I said, as I turned and walked toward the door.

"No problem. Thanks for everything, Doc," the sheriff said as he followed closely behind me. "Ms. Maor, are you okay? You seem way too calm after seeing your sister that way."

"Can we get the fuck out of here, Sheriff? I need to get to my sister's house now," I insisted, pointing at the police car. The sight of shock on the sheriff's face sobered me. "Sheriff, I apologize. There is no time to break down. It's a luxury I don't have. My nephew and my brother-in-law need me. Breaking down right now won't help them, and it won't help me find my sister's murderer," I said, sharply exhaling.

"I get it. Let's get you to your family," Sheriff Alfred replied.

We made our way to the patrol car and pulled away from the coroner's office. The frigid air forced me to ensure the passenger side window was up and firmly in place.

"Jesus, it doesn't get this cold in November in New Orleans. It's still shorts and T-shirt weather there," I said.

"Ms. Maor—"

"Please, Sheriff, call me Nola."

"Nola, I was elected about seven years ago. In that time frame, we've had quite a few missing people. No bodies, just missing people. Like I mentioned before, your sister told me about her identity and who she worked for after I gained her trust. She worked with me, secretly, of course, trying to find some of the people that went missing when they came here. But it always felt like she wasn't telling me the entire story about why she was here, especially for so long. To see her like that… I-I just don't… What was she really investigating?" Sheriff Alfred asked, still visibly shaken from the sight of Janice's body.

"Sheriff, I'm sure my sister shared the basics of her investigations with you, but I know she didn't enlighten you with all the intricacies of them. There's always more to her investigations than meets the eye."

"What do you mean?"

"Meaning there are things in this world that need to be kept in check, away from the eye of the public. Away from your eyes. Let's get to my sister's house. I have a lot of questions, and none of them you can help me with," I said in a monotone voice as I stared at the sheriff.

A partnership with my sister wasn't something I wanted to hear about, especially from some stranger.

"I get it. You're a big time P.I. from New Orleans. Ma'am, I have a job to do. If there's more information you have that can help me find the missing real-estate developer, then I need to know," the sheriff retorted.

"Missing real-estate developer?"

"Yes, some big shot from New York that's here buying up the town. She went missing just a day before the death of your sister."

I glared at Sheriff Alfred and sighed heavily as I shook my head. The car fell quiet as I leaned my head against the head rest.

"Sheriff, it looks as though we may be of some use to each other after all."

Sheriff Alfred accelerated the car down Main Street toward the Williams' household. I decided to put the window back down in the hope that cold air would help numb the pain I felt inside.

CHAPTER 10

The brief walk from Sheriff Alfred's patrol car to the front door of Janice's home provided enough bone-chilling wind to last me a lifetime. The toasty warm atmosphere inside of the Williams' residence was a welcome comfort from the bitter cold on the other side of the door. The cozy warmth inside was pleasing, but I rolled my eyes at the disarray of the living room, then scratched my head.

"What the hell happened in here?" My hand still placed on top of my head with confusion.

Janice's desire to keep a neat and orderly home would create quite the shit storm if she was here to see her house in such a manner.

Darrius stumbled away from the door after he let me inside without speaking a word. He lifted the half empty bottle of amber colored whiskey to his mouth and took what appeared to be another swallow, one of many before, as he made his way to the rear of the house.

"Darrius! Darrius, we should talk about this," I yelled.

His drunken stroll away from me reminded me of the many patrons I've seen stumbling out of a bar on Bourbon Street.

"There's nothing to talk about, Nola," he slurred. Darrius stumbled and stammered against the wall, which inadvertently helped slow him down and kept him on his feet. "She's gone. That fucking job killed my wife. It's going to kill you too." Darrius' large frame tested the resiliency of the drywall as his drunken body repeatedly crashed into it.

Darrius was always a rather large man for as long as I had known him—a former college football player and a standout linebacker that used his football skill to earn a scholarship which paid for his civil engineering degree. Janice used to rave about him to me—and to the entire university campus, for that matter. She constantly bragged about his wit and charm after being together for only a few months. Their love for each other sprouted quickly, and Darrius proposed to Janice during their sophomore year. They had been together ever since.

I always thought about how lucky Janice and Darrius were to have found each other so early in life. To experience that kind of unconditional love with someone other than your parents wasn't afforded to me, yet. I shook my head and tilted it backward in reflection. *I'm not overly optimistic about the potential of finding something like they shared. I suppose it doesn't hurt to be hopeful.*

"Auntie Nola, it's so good to see you."

The gangly built, teenage boy stood near the center of the room. His clothes were wrinkled and unkept. The barely visible bright whiteness of his forced smile contrasted against the earth tone walls and furniture that surrounded him in the open living room. The unexpected thump of his father's bedroom door slamming shut jolted his shoulders in fear, stealing the smile from his face.

"Jackson? My God, boy, you're so tall! It's so good to see you, nephew."

"It's good to see you too, Auntie. Where have you been? Why haven't you come to see us?" he asked timidly. Jackson's eyes were bloodshot red and surrounded with puffy flesh.

"It's complicated, but I haven't forgotten about you. I thought about you a lot. Can we sit down and talk? It's been a very long trip, and I just came from seeing your mother."

I sat on the edge of the sofa, my elbows placed firmly on my knees as I leaned forward. The unfamiliar environment and company of my estranged nephew only stressed my uneasy disposition as my right leg bounced nervously. Jackson sat next to me, I stared into his eyes and saw my sister staring back at me. The light brown irises passed down to him brought back the memories of Janice's nickname of 'Autumn' she carried throughout high school. The name referenced the similarities of the color of her eyes and the fallen leaves from trees on campus. Jackson's other features reflected his father, who already, at the age of fifteen, had a prominent, chiseled, square jawline and spotted facial stubble hair.

"Jackson, your mother and I, we had a complicated re—"

"Auntie, Mama was investigating something," Jackson interrupted. His tone was direct, avoiding the answers to the questions he unloaded on me moments ago. "I don't know what happened to her. From everything she taught me, I'm not sure what could have done that to her, but she was looking for a recent visitor when she died."

"From everything you know?" I raised my eyebrows in surprise. "Jackson, did your mom make you aware of what we do?"

"Yeah, both Dad and I know. She wanted us to know and train. Mama wanted us to be able to defend ourselves. She told me that I needed to know how to defend her future grandkids. So, she started training me a few years ago."

"Janice always did have good foresight. Where is her office? Let's talk more in there and see if we can figure out what the fuck happened and kill whatever it is that did that to your mother."

As I watched the intensity on Jackson's face, his attention focused on every word that passed between my lips. A fleeting crooked smile was momentarily present as he quickly stood. Jackson walked down the nearest hallway, past his parents' bedroom. The cries of his father crept from behind a closed door as we passed.

"Janice! Janice, baby, come back to me," Darrius yelled.

I paused and placed the palm of my hand on the warmth of the wooden door. My hand trembled slightly as I stepped closer to the door. The tip of my boots bumped against the bottom.

"Darrius, I'm going to find out who or what did this to her. They'll pay for this. With God as my witness, I promise they will. I know I've been gone, but I loved Janice deeply. I love you and Jackson too. You don't have to be strong. I'll be strong for you."

"C'mon, Auntie, t-there are some things I want to show you," Jackson interrupted. Tears fell from his eyes, and his voice shook at his father's behavior.

Jackson and I entered Janice's home office. The skin on my arms immediately bumped over from the cold void that was present in the air. The office was the frequent sanctuary of my sister, and it had so many similarities to my own. The walls were lined with bookshelves filled with binders and books of text that provided insight into some of the most vicious beast and demons in the supernatural world. On one wall stood a rather large weapons cabinet with a flare of interior lights, illuminating the selection of deadly artillery.

"The temperature was chilly in her office regardless of the weather outside. The cold air provided a certain comfort for Mama when she was in here using her books, researching and hunting as much evil as she could identify. She showed me some of her old case files. I know she wasn't supposed to, but they were some of the most awesome things I ever saw," Jackson said.

I recalled a conversation with Janice long ago where I concurred with her sentiment of a cold office being optimal for focus. Near the center of the room, I stood next to the desk and stared at the familiar research books and makeshift binders that sat on the nearby bookshelf. A lot of the same texts also sat on the shelves in my own personal library. The sight was almost like a mirror image of my office back home in New Orleans. The similar decor and aesthetic of Janice's office to my own reminded me of our shared taste. A large crevice had formed between us. I had nearly forgotten everything we went through together. How similar we were. My eyes watered as I reflected.

"Mama didn't drink much, but she kept a bottle of whiskey in the drawer of her desk. She told me you enjoyed a drink or two to cope with the stuff you guys see."

"Jackson, I'm not here for that. As a matter of fact, I'm not interested in having a drink at all until I find out what the hell is going on."

"What do you know about what mom was doing here?" Jackson asked as he picked up the assorted papers on the floor.

"Fortunately, the few times we spoke, we still talked about the mission. She was assigned here fifteen years ago to investigate the random disappearances just before you were born. From what your mom told me, she couldn't pinpoint anything corporeal in nature, but there was interesting history and an energy here that seemed unnatural. She said it was simmering like molten magma just beneath the surface, and only God knows what would happen when it erupted."

"Yeah, that was the same fucked up ghost story she told me for many years. Can you imagine hearing that from your Mama? She knew it scared me. She knew all the stories scared me, but she said she wanted me to be prepared."

"Jackson, watch your language. I know my sister raised you with some respect. I'm surprised by my sister's actions to tell you what she did and who we were at such an early age. What were you… twelve when she told you?" I sat in a nearby chair. "That wasn't something she shared with me. When Goliath happened, it shook up our world. People's realities were fractured when the darkness that surrounded them was uncovered. Then your grandparents… She didn't want you to be blind, Jackson."

"Blind? Mama was the one that ended up blind."

"Jackson!"

"I'm sorry! She's gone. She left me. She was the strongest person I knew. Tougher than Dad. What could have done that to her?" Jackson's words slurred as tears fell down his face.

I nervously tugged at the side of my jeans, timidly walked toward Jackson, and wrapped my arms around him. I held him close to my chest and rubbed the top of his closely barbered head, with slow and deliberate strokes to calm him, unsure of myself, and unaware of how to comfort someone in need.

"I'll find out who did this, sweetheart. I promise you. Right now, I need you to pull from that strength your mother and father gave you and tell me everything you know. She made you strong, and I'm going to need that strength to help me put down whatever did this."

Jackson pushed away from me and quickly wiped his tears away. He cleared his throat and exhaled sharply, determined to compose himself.

"M-most of Mama's focus was on the p-plot of land that was the original settlement of this town. That's where all the ddisappearing's seemed to keep happening, and that's where that noise came from that night."

"Wait… a noise?" I interrupted.

"Yeah. The night before we found Mama's body, there was a scream that came from that area. It sounded more like a wail, someone in pain, but it was so loud that it was as if it came from inside the room I was standing in." Jackson sniffed as his voice settled. "It almost sounded like some sort of town siren storm warning system. Everyone I spoke to heard it. Dad heard it too."

"Was that the first time that you or your dad heard it?" I asked.

"Yes. From everything I know, it was the first time anyone had heard it."

"I don't expect it's a coincidence that it happened the night my sister died. Jackson, I want everything—and I mean all the information Janice had—on that settlement camp, the history, the missing persons, anything that happened there until present day, both documented and rumor."

"Well, from what Mama showed me, she always worked out of that orange binder on her desk. These are the files I picked up of the missing persons when we came in. That's all I know about. There may be more on that, but she didn't share it with me yet. But there was the file that was left at the door."

"A file?" I asked.

"Yeah, the day she was… the day she was… the day she was taken from us. Someone left a file with a bunch of stuff in it about this town. We don't know where it came from, but someone dropped it off and left in a big hurry. It's the brown one on the desk."

"That's fine, Jackson. This is a start. Can you tell me why she went to the settlement that night?"

"Well, I don't—"

Behind us, the door crept open. Darrius' oversized, darkened silhouette filled the doorway as the hallway light behind him outlined his massive athletic frame and the large bottle that dangled from his right hand. He stepped inside the office. His eyes were glazed over, and his face with significant unkept hair growth only enhanced unstable look.

"The developer," Darrius mumbled. "Janice went out to investigate the settlement a little more after getting that file. She stayed out there after the sheriff called her and told her the lady was missing since the night before. Some big shot from New York. She went missing while in town on business. She was in town with her executive assistant Tammy... something or another. Jackson and I just finished watching a movie when she called and told me what was going on. From what Janice told me, the developer wanted to make this place the next Black Wall Street or something close to it. She was determined to examine that old settlement thoroughly before committing to plans to change the landscape. The sheriff knows. Find Tammy, start there. Everything you need is in here. This place had something brewing for a long time, according to Janice. I thought she would end it like she ended so many things before. Jackson can help you." Darrius paused and took another couple of swallows from the bottle in his hand. "He's smart and resourceful. Just stay the fuck away from me, please," His words slurred. Darrius slowly turned and stumbled back to his bedroom.

"Auntie, I have to go train. I need to clear my head," Jackson said.

"Go, I've got this. I plan on spending the night right here catching up on Janice's findings and—"

My words came to an abrupt halt after the high-pitched wail bellowed around the room, causing discomfort in my head. The scream intensified, but it was difficult to determine if the source of it was in terrible pain or extremely angry. Jackson and I clutched at our heads, squinting in pain as the involuntary reflex of grinding our teeth added to the muscle tension caused by the auditory assault. The lights in the room emitted a pulsating tone and flickered erratically. The scream abruptly ceased and relieved us of our tortuous infliction.

"My God. Was that it? Is that what you heard, Jackson?" I inquired. My hand rubbed the side of my temple as I attempted to catch my breath.

"Yeah, that was it. No doubt, that was it."

The door to the office once again swung open, and Darrius stood in the doorway.

"Oh, my God. Not again."

CHAPTER 11

The obnoxious laughter of the four young college kids as they entered the lobby of the Dalyville Inn was amplified in the tiny space. The lobby was only about the size of one of those cheap Chinese food takeout restaurants, if they could be called a restaurant at all. Rectangular in shape, the lobby had one old wooden chair in the far-right corner of the room and a single serve coffee machine on the opposite side that sat atop a small table in the other corner of the lobby. The large counter and glass window stretched wall-to-wall for the length of the small, dusty greeting area.

One of the young men aggressively hammered down on the desktop bell, which sat in front of the small opening at the bottom of the glass window. He pushed the sliver of blonde hair that fell in front of his eyes back into place and chugged another few swallows of the cheap can of beer he had down his throat. Dillion crushed the can in his hand when he finished and tossed it to the floor. A loud belch followed. The laughter behind him continued as Dillion again abused the service bell in front of him.

"Who the hell runs this shithole? C'mon, you got customers out here," he yelled.

The slender, bleached blonde young woman behind him wrapped her arm around his waist and leaned her head on the side of his shoulder, her skin cooled by the soft leather of his high school letterman's jacket, the typical sign of a high school athlete reluctant to give up his glory days.

"Dillion, babe, we're only partying for one night. We don't need this shitty motel room. Let's just go to that old settlement and get the party started. We can sleep in one of those old cabins we heard about and be out of here before the hick sheriff even knows we were here," Reagan said, as she clutched the arm of her high school sweetheart.

"Reagan, I don't want to be out in the cold all day. We can party most of the day here in the room, then head toward the settlement for some real fun when the sun goes down. Nobody has to know we're here."

"Sounds like a plan, buddy," Dillion's taller and goofier friend Bruce agreed.

Bruce followed Dillion most of his high school days and still, to this point, as sophomores in college. The once former high school football teammate developed an early kinship with Dillion in the role of the popular Texas high school Quarterback with Bruce protecting his blindside. Bruce was mostly known for his rather thick head and he used that head as his one and only ticket to play football to get into college. Luckily for him, Dillion convinced the University of Nashville to recruit Bruce along with him.

"I like that idea too, baby," Maria replied as she grabbed Bruce around his waist and stood on her toes to kiss him.

Bruce's massive, clumsy fingers stroked Maria's cold black hair. The sounds of their lips intertwining caused Reagan to roll her eyes as Dillion watched with a perverted grin on his face.

"I love you, my little honey," Bruce replied, in his deep voice. The sound of it carried and echoed off the walls.

"Geez, you guys need to get a room," Dillion said, still smirking.

"Oh my God. That's such a lame joke, even for you, babe." Reagan laughed as she slapped Dillion on the chest.

"Yeah, well, we haven't fucking gotten a room yet." Dillon again hammered down on the service bell with his hand.

The lone door behind the counter crept open. Its hinges released a high-pitched squeal as if it was a scream from years of abuse. A wrinkled, liver-spotted hand wrapped around the edge of the door frame as it slowly pushed it open. An old man who wore a dingy, blue gray mechanic's jumpsuit with the name of Reggie stitched on its right side walked up to the service window.

"The fuck do you want?" Reggie's fragile voice cracked as he spoke.

"Are you kidding me, old man? What took your dusty ass so long? We want a goddamn room," Dillion replied.

"What the hell are you piss ants doing in my town, anyway? This ain't no tourist attraction."

"Listen, old man..." Dillon paused to read the name on the jumpsuit. "Reggie, is it? Just give us a room. We don't have time for this Q and A. One room, two queen-sized beds if you have them."

Reggie smiled and displayed a mouth full of rotten black teeth, staring at Reagan as she continued to lean on Dillion. He then lifted the cup in his hand and spit the brownish fluid from his snuff, it had already started to leak down the corner of his mouth.

"You guys are from the university over in Nashville, aren't ya? I bet you came here to see that damn settlement, right?"

"That's none of your business. Just give us a room, please, sir," Reagan said in a soft, polite tone.

Reggie nodded his head toward Maria, bringing attention to the crimson-colored university jacket she wore.

"Hey, is that place really haunted?" Bruce clumsily interrupted.

Reggie's eyes cut toward Bruce, and his smile fell limp. A look of disgust remained as he continued to stare. He glared and turned back toward Reagan as she continued to stare at Reggie's teeth in disbelief.

"You sure do have a purty mouth," Reggie said, once again smiling.

Reagan sheepishly turned away.

"Don't make me fuck you up, Reggie. Just give us the room. We don't have all day. We snuck here to have a little fun away from Nashville. The university doesn't like the students wandering into these small towns out here," Dillion said, stepping as close to the glass barrier as possible.

"Alright, I like you youngins. I remember what it was like at that age. All you wanna do is party and sleep with each other. Room 106 is yours for the night for forty dollars." Reggie slid the key into the slot as Dillion quickly pulled the cash from his pocket. His grin grew larger. "How much do you youngins really like to party? For another forty, I'll throw in this bag of pot and some rolling papers."

"Pot?" Maria laughed and pointed in Reggie's direction.

"Unbelievable. Nobody calls it pot anymore. You mean you have weed, old timer?" Dillion asked, his eye wide with surprise. He pulled more money from his pocket.

"Look at this fuckin place, boy. It's not exactly five stars, is it? I have to earn a livin' some kinda way 'round here."

"Deal," Dillon replied, grabbing the key and the plastic sandwich bag filled with weed from the slot. "I don't need to sign for the room or anything?"

"Have fun, you assholes." The smile on Reggie's face wasn't as wide as before. He nodded as the group turned away from him.

"C'mon, guys, let's get out of here. Place smells like shit." Dillion looked back at Reggie as he walked out the door.

The old man leered back at him with the same creepy grin.

THE GROUP LEFT THE LOBBY, and Reggie spit into his cup one more time. His wrinkled lips curled in disgust as he reached for the phone and quickly dialed a number he had dialed many times before. The phone rang briefly before the voice on the other end spoke.

"Yeah."

"It's me. I got four more. Room 106."

THE PARTY CONTINUED in room 106 at the Dalyville Inn, but eventually slowed as dusk set in. The stained, carpeted floor was covered with empty beer cans and assorted bags of snacks. The room reeked of marijuana, and the empty plastic bag it once sat in lay on the counter. Bruce and Maria lay naked across the bed farthest from the door, unconscious and breathing erratically. Reagan sat in the chair nearest the other bed, now only wearing Dillon's high school letterman jacket and black French cut panties. Her head tilted back, eyes rolled to the back of her head, and also breathing erratically.

Dillion slowly sat up on the bed, with his hand on his forehead as he tried to steady his vision.

"What the hell, man? My head is killing me. What was in that weed?" Dillon mumbled as he stood. "Reagan! Reagan, wake up, baby!"

Reagan moaned in return, still unconscious.

Dillon's legs wobbled when he moved, as if he was a toddler taking his first steps. The room spun as he lost his balance and fell to the floor a few feet from the door. The thunderous sound of the thump against the door caused Dillion to look in its direction. He squinted his eyes and struggled to focus as the door swung open. In the doorway stood the darkened silhouette of a man, with an axe in his hand and a badge on his shirt. Both the axe and the badge twinkled as they caught what little light was left in the room. Dillion reached out to the figure. His hand landed on one of the man's boots as the stranger stepped closer inside. Dillion looked up. The figure lifted the axe, swinging it down upon him and into the back of his head.

CHAPTER 12

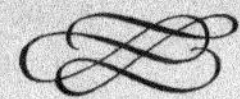

I pulled the curtains apart and peered outside the living room window, gazing upon the icy, glazed grass and trees in the front yard of Janice's home. In disbelief, I had never seen anything this close to snow in person. It was always something only seen on television from my point of view, although Janice used to call and fawn over the beauty of freshly fallen snow. I had to admit; I was always a little jealous. Of course, a little frozen grass wasn't the real thing, but at that point, I would have taken any small sight of joy I could get. The frosted window only provided a hazy, partial view. The towering trees deeply rooted in the front yard, lined up on either side down the driveway, only relinquished filtered sunlight from the sky, but helped maintain the blanket of bitter cold surrounding the home.

"Jesus, Janice. It's freezing here. How could you pick this place? Ugh…I hate the cold. I love the thought of snow, but I hate the cold. You did it for fifteen years, no less," I mumbled, as I sipped from the novelty ceramic coffee mug that featured an animated vampire ironically drinking coffee with the quote 'The REAL life's blood' above its head.

"It's twelve degrees outside. I'm afraid your luck isn't great, Nola. You came in the middle of a nasty cold front. If you're going out, you may want to bundle up a bit," Darrius said. His baritone voice surprised me, forcing my head around to face him. His facial hair was unkept and dark circles had formed under his eyes.

"Darrius, glad to see you up and about. How are you feeling this morning?"

"How do you think I fucking feel, Nola? I have a splitting headache, and I woke up in my bed alone," Darrius snapped, as he sat at the kitchen counter and placed his elbows on the table and his face in his palms. "I'm sorry. I'm sorry. I didn't mean to lash out at you like that."

Darrius walked over to the coffeepot and poured himself a cup, then added whiskey from the small bottle he pulled from his robe pocket.

"Do you think that's a good idea? I know it's hard right now, but Jackson needs you. He needs me. Most of all, he will need both his father and auntie sober and there to help him get through this tough time."

Darrius scoffed, turning his head away. "Are you kidding me? You know how close your sister and I were? She told me about your… shall we say… dependence on the sauce. Now you're lecturing me on drinking and being strong? Janice was every-thing to me."

"You are making an ass out of yourself. Now isn't the time to take jabs at me. I know I have my problem, but we're talking about you right now. Janice was everything to me, too. You don't think I want to break down right now? Just go in a room and bury my sorrows in a pillow and a bottle?" I yelled, and my hands trembled once again. "I get it. Janice was your soulmate. No doubt about it, but she wasn't everything. She gave you a son. A son that needs his father after losing the most important woman in his life. He needs you to be the strong man you've shown him you are. You can't fall apart right now," I pleaded.

I leaned slightly forward and took one small step toward him. I rubbed my hands together, anxious, and I slowly opened my arms to embrace him.

Thoughts of the past flashed through my head. I briefly remembered the type of person I was a long time ago. It had been so long since I held another human being, in any manner that meant anything. I wasn't sure I still knew how to do it. So much time had passed, and I had been so closed off. I couldn't remember how to comfort another person, how to be open...to be human.

Darrius stared at me, one eyebrow raised, and poured more of the liquid courage into his mug. His eyes watered, and tears fell down his face as his eyes shifted down to his mug. His hands shook as he walked up to me and reached his arms out timidly with looks of uncertainty. Unsure if I would embrace him, Darrius paused and stood in front of me, then exhaled sharply as he glared into my eyes. He didn't force it. Which, at some level, I hoped he would. His expression filled with pain.

"Take the car. It's a small town, but you'll need it to get around fast and to get to the original settlement," he said as he walked off back toward his bedroom. "Nola, find whatever did this to my wife and finish it. Kill it. If you don't, I will, at all costs." Darrius slammed the bedroom door closed behind him.

THE OLD HABIT of knocking on strangers' doors, unexpected to them, was one of the few aspects of being a New Orleans police detective I carried over into my private investigator's career. People were more unlikely to keep their lies straight and much more easily manipulated to pull any information from them if it was hidden. I continued to aggressively knock against the chipped white paint on the motel room door. The sound echoed throughout the open breezeway. The discomfort of the pounding with my hand left slight white scratches upon the dried-out skin on my knuckles, already being assaulted by the cold Tennessee air.

Jesus, Nola, that stings. Why didn't you put on gloves?

As the door opened after some of my best well developed urgent knocking, accompanied by an authoritative voice, a thinly framed, pale skinned, and well-dressed woman answered.

She swung the door open abruptly.

"Who the hell do you think you are knocking at—" The woman's indignant tone came to a crashing halt at the sight of the rather tall woman standing in the doorway.

The dripping essence of authority in my demeanor was only eclipsed by the stern look in my eyes and the prominent scar that reached diagonally across my jawline.

"Ms. Tammy Hodges, I presume. I'm Nola Maor. I'm a private investigator out of New Orleans. Do you mind if we speak for a few minutes?"

"Umm… sure. All the way from New Orleans? What can I do for you?"

"I have some information, which tells me that your boss has been missing for a couple of days now. Do you mind telling me what happened?"

"I don't understand. Why would a private investigator from New Orleans be interested in a missing person's case in Tennessee for a woman who's from New York?" Tammy asked, her northeast no-nonsense attitude reaffirming itself.

"The sheriff knows I'm here and… Look, are you familiar with the name Janice Williams?"

"Yes, I heard about her unfortunate death. There were some weird circumstances surrounding it, I heard. I don't know much about it, just what I overheard the people in the diner gossiping about. What does that have to do with me or Ms. Jones?"

"Janice Williams was my sister and a former FBI agent. She and the sheriff were the ones who started looking for Ms. Jones after her unexpected disappearance. Now she's dead. Does that spark your curiosity?" I asked, slightly raising one brow and twisting up the corner of the left side of my mouth.

After my line of questioning, my pocket vibrated feverishly as my phone rang inside. I reached in to retrieve it, only to see the screen illuminated by another 'Unknown Caller' message. The ringing halted with the message popping up which read 'one missed call'. I placed the phone back into my pocket.

Tammy stepped outside and fastened the top button on her suit blazer. Unusually fully dressed at eight o'clock in the morning, apparently, she wasn't a woman to lounge around during any part of the day. Even I would admit it took a certain personality type that would get up immediately in the morning, get fully dressed in some type of suit, and be completely ready to go when an unexpected stranger knocks at the door.

"I'd much rather speak out here, Ms. Maor. I've been a little cooped up lately inside that god-awful motel room. It reeks of cigarette stench. Although I don't particularly know you, I would be glad to talk to you. Somebody has to figure out what's going on here and tell me Ms. Jones's whereabouts. It's already been two days and at this point she is either hurt terribly or something far worse has happened."

"Someone brought me up to speed on what you ladies are doing here. I know about the investors and the vision Ms. Jones has for the town. It sounds promising. Enough to rival Nashville in a couple of decades, I think." My eyebrows raised in approval. "My question is when did you last see Ms. Jones?"

"We've been here for almost five days now. This town and its people have issues with us being here. Of course, anyone would expect that. Most people are resistant to change. It's just… they're on the strange side, especially when it comes to the piece of land located a little on the outskirts of Main Street." Tammy replied.

"You mean the original settlement of Dalyville?" I asked.

"Yes, Ms. Jones had been undecided about how she wanted to handle it. Make it a tourist center, business park, or just tear it all down and build an additional subdivision. I've never seen her struggle with a decision like this before. She's usually very decisive. Not this time, though. This time, she actually wanted to wait for her project manager, Charles Jones, to run some ideas by him." Tammy shook her head in confusion. "She said it was because of some information she found out about the history of the settlement recently, but it didn't seem that way. It seems like she had this knowledge beforehand. I've worked closely with Ms. Jones for quite a while, and her demeanor was calm and calculated. Usually, when she has new information, her blood gets going, and she's pretty hyper. Whatever it was, it shook her up a bit, but she didn't elaborate."

I focused in on Tammy's words as they passed her lips. A tiny chill traveled down my spine as I listened to Tammy's comment about the town's history.

"What does that have to do with the night you last saw Ms. Jones?" I pushed.

Tammy's eyes widened at the question, hesitant in her response. "W-well, we had just come back to the motel after another cholesterol filled meal from that pink, grease trap diner down the road. Ms. Jones told me she was going back to the settlement to see if she could get some inspiration and come to a decision. She almost seemed a little desperate to get there and decided to walk down to the sheriff's station to get a ride or escort—"

"You don't belong here," the frail, shaky voice came from an older man inserting himself into the conversation.

The man stood only a few feet away from Ms. Tammy and me. His ratty denim jumpsuit barely covered the discolored white T-shirt underneath. "None of you belong here. We don't like your kind here. All you do is bring trouble," he continued. His frail, wrinkled fingers white knuckled the push broom in his hand.

I dipped my head and exhaled sharply in frustration. I turned and walked toward the old man. Even someone at his age I preferred not to be off guard while I stood next to him. You never know what wolf lies dormant in sheep's clothing. The familiar stench of alcohol emanated from the pores of his skin.

"What's your name, old timer?" I asked.

"My name doesn't matter, girly. You and your carpetbagger friend need to get out of here before you end up missing like that other black girly."

"Excuse me!" Tammy yelled.

I grabbed handfuls of the denim overalls on the old man and pinned him against the door of the probable empty neighboring room. A weak and frail laugh followed with a barrage of mucus filled coughs came from the old man as he tried to catch his breath from the force I pushed him with, knocking the wind out of him. The reek stench of his breath instantly made me regret my hot-headed decision to rough him up. I glanced down at his overalls and noticed the name Reggie stenciled on the front.

"You have some information you'd like to share, Reggie?" I asked.

"She should have left. Just like you two girlies should. I saw her. I saw her and the deputy leave that night. I knew where they were going. I knew they didn't want her here," the old man said. His grin was barely present, smothered by his overgrown and unkept mustache.

"Shit, man. You're a walking, talking cliche right out of an 80s slasher movie." I relaxed my grip and took a step away from him. "Where were they going, and who didn't want her here? What fucking deputy?"

The rapid back-to-back blare of a police siren and the rev down of the engine interrupted the line of questioning I had. Sheriff Alfred stepped out of the car quickly and approached us.

"Hey, Reggie, get the hell out of here and leave these ladies alone, you asshole. I'm sure there's plenty you have to do right now," Alfred said, while removing his wide-brimmed hat. His brow was moist, as if it was the dead of summer. "Nola, we need to go to the settlement grounds. We've had another murder. Ms. Hodges, I'm going to need you to come with us too."

"Sheriff, you mind telling us what the hell is going on? Why do you look like you've seen a ghost?"

"I don't know what the hell is going on, but I'm to the point where I'm not ruling ghosts out either. Deputy Farley is dead.

We found him at the settlement. His skin is gray, and his eyes are missing. They leaked that nasty black fluid. Just like your sister."

As I listened to the words pass his lips, my eyes widen and affixed on the sheriff. My heart thumped in my chest as I listened to the sheriff describe the gruesome details of the deputy's body.

"You go ahead without me. I'll have Tammy show me the way there. I have to make a stop first," I said, firmly. "Somebody has some questions to answer."

CHAPTER 13

I pulled into the parking lot of the Dalyville Diner. The off-street parking only had a few pickup trucks scattered about in parking spaces. The aesthetics of buildings weren't usually something I cared much about, but the sight of the hot pink color was offensive to my eyes. Almost as offensive as someone putting pineapples on pizza…almost.

"Thank you for taking the quick ride, Tammy. I tend to rub people the wrong way when I question them, and sometimes things can escalate. I need you to wait here in the car, and we'll head to the old settlement when I get back," I said.

I pulled Corbin from my holster, and with a quick spin of the barrel, I ensured a round was in every chamber.

Tammy cut her eyes toward the driver's side seat and stared at Corbin, with her eyebrows raised. I re-holstered it under my coat.

"Nola, I think I'm perfectly fine waiting here for you to come back." Tammy pushed her glasses back firmly on the bridge of her nose with the tip of her finger.

The signs posted in the window still had a brightness to them that complemented the pink structure that housed them. Double glass doors hugged by large pane windows gave the rickety diner a rather cozy, small-town feel. Given its location, the owners probably didn't have to try very hard to achieve the desired atmosphere. First impressions of the exterior left me little hope that the owners of this place made its kitchen hygiene their first priority. The window-based marketing seemed to be the owner's personal passion project. Tacky would be the word I was looking for.

"Home of the world's best pork stew! Nobody knows pork like a pig farmer. Grab a hearty bowl that will keep you full all day long!" The signs read as I approached the door. Not very poetic, but straight to the point. I had the feeling that the flavor claims of the stew wouldn't hold up to the first-rate flavor festivals of New Orleans cuisine. Satisfying an appetite wasn't a priority, anyway. Tammy mentioned this was the place Janice and Ms. Jones met when they came into town. It should at least give me an idea if the conversation between the two seemed normal enough or if there was anything unusual about it.

As I walked inside, my presence garnered most of the patrons' attention as they turned their heads in my direction. It reminded me of those old western movies when the stranger walked into the tavern, and all the card-playing patrons turned and stared. This was far from the small-town southern hospitality that so many southern people like to brag about. The stares were anything but welcoming. Hanging on the wall to my right was an old photo of a couple that could easily have been in their 80s when it was taken. It appeared to be a married couple, but after I stared at it for a few seconds, while everyone still gawked in my direction, I recognized what the photo was. I couldn't believe it was displayed in a diner of all places. The dead look in the couple's eyes as their bodies were propped up in chairs made it obvious what the photo was and the poor taste of the person who decided to display it here.

"Death photo," the sweet-sounding southern accent shouted from behind the diner's counter. "Those were the great-grand-parents of the current mayor of this charming little town and the grandchildren of the founders of this slice of America you visited. Is there something we can do for you, darlin'? Are you hungry?" the husky lady in the pink waitress uniform asked as she smiled in my direction.

The small group of people seated inside still glared in my direc-tion. To call it a sparse crowd would be generous. Only about seven in total. Given the creep factor of the place, it wasn't something I couldn't handle if things took a turn for the worse. Although the thickly built blonde lady with the sweet voice greeted me with a welcoming, warm and bright smile, the couple that sat at the far end of the counter made it obvious I was not welcomed.

A man with a heavy frame, thin gray hair, and salt-and-pepper goatee stared at me with his deep ocean blue eyes in a manner that didn't seem to have the best intention. The woman next to him twisted her stringy brown hair with her finger, looked at me with disgust, and curled up her excessively wrinkled lips.

Life had taken a physical toll on both of them, and from the looks of it, most likely from harboring loads of anger. Most of the others seemed ordinary.

"I'm not hungry at the moment," I replied.

"Are you sure? We have three things on the menu that we do exceptionally well. Donald back there in the kitchen makes a mean cheeseburger and fries, a thick and juicy smothered chicken breast, and of course our world-famous pork stew that's just full of tender and juicy pork cutlets, vegetables and a blend of southern seasonings to die for. Best you'll ever have. The name is Sissy by the way. Jessie, why don't you seat our guest at a table and give her a menu?"

Sissy nodded at the attractive young lady with the white blouse and name tag on her shirt.

"No thanks, Sissy. I'm curious, though. How does a small diner in such a small town get the crown for world's best stew? You guys win a contest or something?" I asked in a bit of a snarky tone.

My eyes drifted away from Sissy and back to the snarling couple, who still glared at me. Each had a large bowl in front of them, which I assumed was the stew.

Sissy's laugh filled the diner after she heard the comment. "No, darlin'. This town is our world, and the townsfolk love it. That's why it's the world's greatest stew. So, if you're not here to eat, then what can we do for you?"

"Ma'am, a few days ago, my sister and another visitor in town had lunch in your establishment. You might have seen them.

They're two African American ladies. One is a resident of your town. Her name is Janice. I wanted to know if there was anything unusual about their conversation?"

"Oh, honey, we all know Janice. So sorry to hear about her unfortunate passing," Sissy said. The smile on her face remained plastered in place.

An unexpected laugh erupted from the far end of the counter. The aged lady with the stringy brown hair grinned, and her discolored teeth made an appearance. A thinly built man that sat at a table not far from the couple at the counter stopped eating and looked up in my direction. His eyes fixed on me. I walked over toward another man that sat at the counter in closer proximity to me. His head pointed down toward the plate in front of him. A baseball cap covered his eyes as he cut his chicken breast with a steak knife and stuffed it in his jaws with the fork.

"Is there something funny, miss? I asked a simple question," I inquired. My brow furrowed with confusion.

"Look here, girly. Don't nobody 'round here care about your dead sister or any outsider that don't belong. The fact that you wandered in here askin' about it like they mattered is funny to me. I gather it's funny to everybody else in here, too." The vile woman smiled at me as if she took satisfaction in any frustration I showed.

"Jean, hush now! This lady is just trying to see if we can help her out. I'm sure she's not lookin' for no trouble."

"Sissy, I know damn well you didn't just 'hush' me like I'm your child. You might be better off if you stayed in your place."

The smile on Sissy's face disappeared as she took a couple of steps back away from the counter and leaned against the prep counter where the chef put the readied orders through the kitchen window. Jean looked back at her bowl of stew and ate a couple more spoonfuls.

The sight of the woman briefly became blurry. My hands shook, and my breaths felt labored. I tried to steady my hands as I pressed them firmly on the service counter. The patron next to me still shoveled food into his mouth with his fork, unconcerned with what was happening.

"Jean, is it? Jean, how about you keep your goddamn mouth shut, and let these people offer a helping hand if they want?" I asked as my breathing steadied and my vision quickly cleared.

"Look here, bitch—" Jean yelled.

I grabbed the steak knife from the plate of the man next to me and threw it in the direction of the couple on the other end of the counter. The knife sliced through the air, flipping end over end near the head of Jean, and planted into the wall behind the couple. The thin man that sat at the table behind them hurriedly stood. A bulge on his right side, under his oversized T-shirt, sat just at the waistline of his blue jeans.

The heavyset man next to Jean extended his hand out. His palm faced in the direction of the man now standing at the table, catching his attention. With his arm extended, I noticed the tattoo etched into his forearm. An inverted pentagram enclosed in a circle and centered between two crescent moons. A slight twist to the more traditional witchcraft symbol. My hands continued to shake after throwing the knife.

"There's no need." The heavyset man said as his deep blue, ocean-colored eyes fixed on me.

The thin man sat back down at the table and finished eating.

"Kill that bitch, Jerry!" Jean yelled.

"Now. Now, Jean. We won't be doin' anything like that," he said as he focused his attention on me again. "You say your name is Nola, right? Well, Nola, I'm Jerrious Daly. Folks call me Jerry, and I'm the mayor of this fine town. Now, truth is I was here the day your sister and that carpetbagger sat in here and had lunch. We're still trying to get the smell out just from them being in here. They sat. They ate. They talked. Then they both left. We don't give a fuck about what happened after they left here. We also don't care about what happened to your sister. Even after all these years of living here, she was still an outsider. You're an outsider, and if you know what's best for you, you'll leave."

As I looked at the faces around the room, I realized I uncovered about as much information as I could get from these people. The waitress was the only person with fear on her face. The cook peered over the service counter at what was taking place.

"Oh, I'll be leaving this diner, Jerry, but I'm not going anywhere. Not until I find out what the hell is going on around here and what exactly happened to my sister. Sissy, thank you for your hospitality," I said as I turned and walked out the door.

The cold air again assaulted my sensibilities and reminded me that I was outside my element and outside of my comfort zone. My hands steadied as I drove away toward the sheriff's station, with Tammy in tow in the passenger seat. After that encounter, only one question ate away at me.

"Janice, what the hell kind of place have you been living in these past fifteen years?"

"Was it that bad inside?" Tammy asked.

"You have no idea."

CHAPTER 14

The yellow caution tape flapped violently in the wind. I exhaled sharply and shook my head at the sight of the caution tape and the burn of the frigid air in my nostrils. Over the years, working for the police department and hunting some of the most vicious creatures that tore through New Orleans, the neon yellow of the caution tape became synonymous with death at every crime scene. The damned cold weather didn't make the situation any more comfortable.

The uniformed body of the deputy lay unnaturally stiff in a fetal position and looked less human the closer I approached. Usually, a body in this horrific condition raised a ton of questions and probably would have made me sick in my earlier law enforcement years. This was a far cry from those days of gun shot and stab wounds. It was Goliath that pulled the veil, showing the darkness that blanketed the world and hardened me to its tragedies.

Although it seemed New Orleans had become a little more comfortable and blind again to the darkness in the city. New Orleans was always comfortable in its supernatural lore, accompanied with the party lifestyle, it helped people conveniently forget what was out there. It wasn't often I would have so much company on my investigations, but with so many questions still unanswered about Janice and the whereabouts of Ms. Jones, I would take any help I could get to find answers to my questions.

"Deputy Shannon, this is Nola Maor, the specialist I mentioned. And you're already familiar with Tammy Hodges, our missing person's assistant," Sheriff Alfred said.

"Damn, lady. That's a hell of a scar you got there on your face. How in the hell did you get that?" Shannon fixed his eyes on the right side of my face.

"Your mother gets feral at night when I go in my basement to feed her. The old dog is quite a handful," I stared at the deputy with a raised eyebrow and a smirk.

Deputy Shannon nodded in acknowledgment and raised his brow as he glared at the sheriff. "Sir, do you mind if I talk to you a minute?" He walked a few feet away.

The sheriff followed closely.

"Sir, why do we need them to help investigate the murder of one of our own? What makes her so special?"

"Shannon, I understand your frustration. You have a co-worker, who was a friend, mutilated on the ground in front of you.

Have you ever seen anything like this before? I'll answer that for you. No! You haven't. Why was he out here? Do you know?"

The sheriff's stern scowl forced the deputy to avert his eyes.

"I didn't think so. Let me do my job, and you do yours—while you still have one. By the way, where the hell is Deputy Westin?"

Deputy Shannon shrugged his shoulders and veered his eyes away from the sheriff again. There wasn't much that stood out about the deputy. He was a little taller than the average man, not quite thin with cold black hair slicked back with enough hair gel that could help start a campfire if we needed before we froze to death out in this bitter cold air.

"Fuck if I know. I've been trying to reach him by radio and his cell phone all morning. No luck."

I made my way under the caution tape and stood only a couple of feet from the body after overhearing the sheriff's conversation with Deputy Shannon. Arms still and by my sides, I inhaled deeply and stared down at my boots. My focus heightened as my perception of everything around me slowed. That caution tape went from flapping violently in the wind to a gentle, slow rocking caused by a breeze. My steps around the body were deliberate as the minuscule spacing between them allowed me to soak in more of the crime scene, while I scanned it all with my eyes.

Deputy Farley's withered body lay on its side, with his once snug-fitting uniform hanging loosely from his frame. The deathly, hoary skin was similar to the color of the menacing sky, as a severe storm seemed to approach. My skin bumped over when I stared into the black void of his ocular cavities and inspected the still dripping black sludge that seeped from them. The sunken flesh that surrounded Deputy Farley's facial bone structures reflected complete terror on his face, and his neck contorted unnaturally.

I felt Tammy's gaze as I examined the deputy's body without a flinch or sign of hesitation. Tammy, on the other hand, must have had an almost uncontrollable and gripping sensation of nausea as she covered her agape mouth, the other pressed against her stomach.

I'm sure that as a lifelong New York City resident the sight of a body lying in the street was nothing new to her.

I could only assume it was the grotesque nature of the body, paired with the creepy vibe of the small settlement that gripped her insides and caused such a reaction.

"What are you looking for?" Tammy asked. She wiped away the last of the vomit from her mouth.

"Ms. Hodges, I'm not sure if you're in tune with some of the more unnatural things that are out there, but certain phenomenon has a very ritualistic way of killing their prey. Right now, I'm trying to support the hunch I have."

"Phenomenon? What on earth are you talking about?" Tammy asked.

"Exactly what I said. You don't read the news much, do you? I'm not surprised. I take it most of your downtime is spent reading about all things real-estate or business," I replied.

Tammy rolled her eyes with agitation, shooting me a look of annoyance in return.

"That's not a knock against you, Tammy. I do the same with my profession. The incidents I'm referring to are usually buried in the back pages of the newspaper now and covered up with some sort of narrative that leaves the events as unexplained. Those incidents never make the five o'clock news anymore, and people like you who aren't paying close attention don't give what they read or hear a second thought."

Tammy widened her eyes as she listened to me preach about people's apathy.

"Wait, Nola Maor… and you're from New Orleans. I remember now. There was some sort of incident with a serial murderer and creature or something about fifteen years ago. There was a cop who was responsible for putting an end to all of it. It was all over the news, but I remember us New Yorkers still thought it was some sort of hoax. You were that cop, weren't you?"

I looked away and focused back on the body to avoid her question. The sheriff and deputy stared at me after Tammy's spirited recollection.

"Tammy, was this the deputy Ms. Jones tried to get to escort her here?" I asked.

"I'm not sure. I didn't see a face or a car," Tammy replied, shaking her head.

"It had to have been him. It wasn't me. Unless it was Westin, but he went to Nashville earlier that day for some sort of date. He planned on staying there overnight," Deputy Shannon inserted.

Sheriff Alfred tilted his head and asked, "If you didn't see a face or a car, how can you be sure it was one of my deputies that escorted Ms. Jones?"

"I'm not sure, Sheriff. I can only tell you what Ms. Jones told me." Tammy shrugged. "What I do know is she wouldn't get into a car with some unknown resident of this small town, and she definitely wouldn't walk the few miles to get here. Especially at night and in the cold."

"Well, there are only three deputies in my department. If it wasn't Deputy Shannon, then it had to be Deputy Westin or Deputy Farley. Since he's here, I'd say it must have been Farley," the sheriff answered.

"Perhaps, Sheriff, but let's not jump to conclusions just yet. He could've been here, still searching for her. If Deputy Farley was responsible, why would he come back here?" I inserted.

The stiff body on the ground didn't give me much more to go on. I looked around at the old wooden structures of the settlement. The well was only a couple of dozen feet away. The thick coating of dirt and mud that accumulated over the years mixed with the well's red brick that was still prominent. My gaze lingered on the well longer than I wanted, given the eerie feeling it gave me. After I turned away from the sight of it, I gazed back at Deputy Farley and the lifeless void that was his body.

There was no violence enacted upon it, except for his broken neck. He had no cuts. No scratches. No bruises. It was as if he was caught by surprise and simply drained of his life-force.

"Sheriff Alfred and Deputy Shannon, I don't want you to think I'm being insulting toward you, but I need to have a frank discussion about your town. How much do you know about its history?" I asked.

"I know what most of the town knows. Two families led the settlement from Ireland and originally settled here with five other families. One of the families didn't agree with where they settled, and it caused some friction within the community," Deputy Shannon said. He waved his hands around as if he had told the story dozens of times before. "Eventually, the lead family, the Gallaghers, died off. Then, the other family, the Dalys, moved the settlement a few miles down the road to where the town is now. Just a bunch of farmers."

I gave Shannon a repugnant look and shook my head in disbelief, while I walked closer to the well to canvass for evidence.

"Deputy, I'm not sure if that's what you believe, or you purposefully told some sanitized version because of the company you have. There's a lot more to this little town than what's on the surface. I've only been here two days and have learned a lot about the blood this town was founded on," I said.

I approached the well away from the others.

After a quick glance at one another, the others followed me as their curiosity got the best of them.

"That was everything I learned about it," Deputy Shannon rebutted.

"Unfortunately, there's more to the story, Deputy," the sheriff interjected.

I stared at the sheriff with a slight grin after he gave his answer to the deputy. I dragged my fingertip along the top bricks of the well.

"The sheriff knows most of what I'm about to tell you. Well, maybe. My sister moved here over fifteen years ago on assignment for the FBI. She was investigating the history of this town, among other strange things that seemed to happen in the area. She gathered a lot of information through research since she's been here. Since I've been in town, I've read every page of the research my sister had on the history of Dalyville, along with a little unexpected information that fell in my lap."

Deputy Shannon glared over at the sheriff.

"How could you keep this from your deputies, boss? You kept us in the dark about an investigation going on in the town? Was it centered around the people that went missing here in the area? Because we could have used her help and the resources of the Feds to find out what the hell is happening," Shannon snapped, stepping toward the sheriff with his finger extended.

"There is a little more to it, Deputy. Janice was helping with that, but she also had other investigative responsibilities. There wasn't much evidence to work with. It was as if those people just vanished. Not even their belongings were left behind. It's why she and the bureau felt it had something to do with this settlement." Sheriff Alfred glanced in my direction.

I nodded for him to continue.

"Given his lackluster answer previously, I don't think the deputy knows all the facts about the families. Of the seven families that settled the land, the more well-off of the two lead families, the Gallaghers, owned a slave—a young girl. Well, they really weren't wealthy at all. They just had more than the other families they settled with. Eventually, after a few weeks, the land was settled, and the well was dug," the sheriff said.

"The slave girl and the daughter of the other family, the Daly's, were close in age and became friends. The Daly girl treated her like an equal for some reason, and it was told that because of that, she couldn't tolerate being a slave anymore. I don't believe that part, because who can tolerate the humility and brutality of slavery in the first goddamn place? She murdered her master and his wife in their sleep. She ran, and the townsfolk found her and lynched her. Then they moved the settlement to the land that the Dalys thought would be more bountiful. That's the gist of it. Pretty tragic beginnings for the town," Sheriff Alfred said, sharing the history as he knew it.

I grinned at the sheriff, slightly impressed, and continued to investigate the details of the scene.

"I don't believe it," Deputy Shannon responded. "Why would the town keep that hidden? It seems to me that should be remembered."

"That's horrific," Tammy added, with her head lowered. "Does anyone know any more about the young girl or even a little more about the Gallaghers? Why would they have someone enslaved, given how the Irish were treated in this country?"

"Ms. Hodges, there's a sad history of assimilation on those Irish settler's part. A lot of them took jobs as overseers on plantations to get more acceptance in society. I'm not sure what the young, enslaved girl's name was, or if there was much more information about her or the Gallaghers." Sheriff Alfred shrugged his shoulders.

"Pretty close, Sheriff. Not quite all the horrific details, either." I paused and peered down into the blackness inside the well. "Sheriff, how long has this well been decommissioned? I can't see the bottom, of course, but..." I retrieved a nearby stick from the ground and tossed it inside. I could hear it hit the bottom. "There's no splash or sign of water."

"From what I've been told, before moving the settlement, the families sealed off the stream underneath with brick. Partying college kids have used it as a trash bin every so often. We run them off when we catch them here," he replied. He removed his hat from his head, slapping it against the side of his leg as he sighed. "You know, ma'am, I'm starting to agree with the deputy a little here. What does any of this have to do with the murder of one of my officers?"

I bent over the edge of the well; my torso hung over into the interior and my feet actively struggled to maintain their grip on the ground.

"Jesus Christ, what are you doing?" Tammy yelled. She grabbed the back of my shirt and top of my jeans as she tried to pull me back up.

Two oddly shaped bricks only a couple of feet from the top of the well's edge caught my attention. I rubbed the layers of dust and debris away from the bricks and felt like sporadic indenta-tions on them. The clearing of the dirt revealed the missing piece of a puzzle I had in my mind about the odd circumstances of the town. The indentations weren't sporadic at all, but a pattern.

"Tammy, can you reach the notepad sticking out of my back pocket?" I asked.

Tammy retrieved the notepad and placed it in my hand as I blindly reached back. I glanced over my shoulder and saw Tammy looking back at me with raised eyebrows and her head tilted. She watched as I placed one sheet of paper from the notepad against the brick and quickly rubbed the black tipped pencil back and forth across it. I glanced at the symbols from the impression and flipped the notepad closed. Tammy pulled at my jeans and assisted me as I stood up from the well. I brushed away any remaining dirt from my clothing; a wide grin planted upon my face.

"Well, Sheriff, your variation of the story is still rather PG, I'm afraid. The details are much more morbid and tragic. From what I believe I just found in that well, your deputy's death has a part in this." I moved a little closer to everyone.

Furrowed brows were shared among the three faces as I spoke.

"Where are you going with this, Nola?" Sheriff Alfred asked with a heavy sigh.

"When those families came over from Ireland, you were right, Sheriff. There was one family that had a little more money than the rest, and they did have a teenage slave girl. Her name was Hannah, and she was pregnant. Just as you said, she was also friends with the daughter of the Dalys, the second family. A bit more than friends, I should say. They were in love, and they did an excellent job of hiding it, for a while."

"Mrs. Gallagher, I'm afraid, wasn't happy about the fair color of Hannah's son when he was born a couple of months later. She forced Mr. Gallagher to sell the child and ripped him from Hannah's arms. Hannah never recovered from it, finding her only comfort in the love she had nurtured with the Daly's daughter, Fiadh. Fiadh did her best to comfort Hannah, and for the most part, their love grew stronger during that time, raising the suspicions of the townspeople."

"The Dalys kept their daughter away from Hannah because of the rumors. An act that Janice believes sent Hannah over the edge. One night, she snuck from her tiny slave quarters and into the master's bedroom armed with an axe. Hannah quietly made her way inside and buried the axe in both the master's and mistress' skull. She fled that night but refused to run too far away from her love. The next morning, the townsfolk put together a search party and found Hannah hiding in the woods. They tied her up and dragged her back to the settlement tied to a horse. By the time they made it back, pieces of flesh were torn from her."

"Once they reached the settlement, they lynched her and threw her body down this well, along with the bodies of the Gallaghers. The father of the Daly family led that lynching, most likely out of pure disgust for his daughter and his hatred of the Gallaghers. They later sealed the well, re-routed the water and left the bodies in this dark pit of hatred and despair."

Both the sheriff and Tammy stood with their mouths open, and eyes billowed. Deputy Shannon had his face in his palms. These vicious acts of hate were jarring when heard for the first time. Especially to those in denial of it or those who related to it. My suspicion was that Tammy knew the struggles of hateful glares because of the person she loved. The manner in which she spoke of Ms. Jones seemed to be more than envy. Tammy's eyes watered as she held her head down.

"Christ, almighty, that's terrible," Sheriff Alfred mumbled. "I don't mean to be insensitive, but what does any of this have to do with the murders of your sister and Deputy Farley? What could have done that to them?"

"There was one thing my sister missed, Sheriff. The Daly family had a secret. I only found it because of the tattoo on their descendant's arm I noticed in the diner. It was a Triquetra. They were a family of witches. At least, I suspect the mother and daughter were. That symbol on his arm was a popular symbol of witchcraft, although it was slightly twisted from the original." I rubbed the cover of the notepad with my thumbs. "So, I suspected that sometime before Hannah's murder, she and Fiadh left a marking on this well. This marking can manifest some vicious things if used improperly," I said as I held up the notepad and showed them the etching.

"Are you serious? Witchcraft? I'm having a hard time believing this, Ms. Maor," Tammy said.

"Believe it or not, Ms. Hodges, but right now, we need to get the deputy's body to the morgue, find Ms. Jones as soon as possible, and most of all, get back to the new settlement before dark. All that evil and blood from the past centered on this well. A well, marked by a witch that used this as a symbol of her love for another. This is a desecrated grave site and something or someone released an evil that had been sleeping."

"This all seems a little out there for me," Tammy replied.

"I'll explain the symbol when we get back to the sheriff's station, but we need to leave…now."

CHAPTER 15

T he toasty warmth and comfort of the sheriff's station was a welcome change from the wind and frigid atmosphere of the original settlement and greasy repulsive setting of that diner. It had been a while since I was inside any type of police station. I avoided them. For the most part, they all shared similar layouts. Even the Dalyville Sheriff's Station was no different, although the rough years of the small town had taken its toll on the station as well. The timeworn wooden benches of the waiting area and large U-shaped sergeant's desk were just as ugly as the faded yellow paint.

Usually, if there were questions by the upper brass in New Orleans, they met me on the scene of an incident or preferred to come to my office, so they wouldn't be seen. The conversations almost always went one of two ways: what supernatural forces caused the bloodshed on some unexplained crime scene, or if was I interested in wearing the shield again? The answer was always no to the latter. I knew the leadership of my former employer enjoyed their plausible deniability, and I could never do the job the way it needed to be done under the watchful eye of the badge. The prolonged absence of wearing the badge no longer gave me a feeling of safety or purpose when I entered a police station. Tonight, was an exception.

"Okay, Nola. You have our attention. Deputy Farley is at the morgue, and we're probably in the safest place in town, before or after dark. Your story of the original families caught me off guard, but I get the feeling there's more to it. What is it you aren't telling us?" Sheriff Alfred raised his brow as he fiddled with the brim of his hat, unnerved by the information he recently learned about his hometown.

"It's not just some story, Sheriff. It's all accounted for in the ledgers and diaries my sister collected and found. That history and this symbol explain why there was so much uneasiness and energy surrounding that place."

I held up the impression I took from the well. Their eyes darted in its direction.

"Forgive me, but what does that have to do with Ms. Jones? It seems you're here on some monster hunt, while my boss is still missing. What are we going to do to find her?" Tammy added.

The high-pitched tone of her voice contradicted her well put together demeanor. I often forget how some of these sights can affect people. Their reality breaks when exposed to the super-natural world. With Tammy, I'm reminded of how she reacted to the view of the deputy's disfigured body.

"My sister is dead." I said in a softer tone. "This isn't a game. The only way this works is if we understand the truth of everything and everyone involved in it. It's not a monster hunt, at least not yet. Anyway, if my instincts are right, all the events, past and present, are connected," I replied, as I lowered my notepad in frustration and placed it into my back pocket. "Tammy, you said that Ms. Jones was looking for a ride to the settlement, specifically from one of the deputies. She then goes missing and deputy Farley ends up dead at Ms. Jones's desired destination in a gruesome way. Why? Sheriff, I doubt you have patrols out there and who would want to go out there for the hell of it?"

The sheriff and Deputy Shannon both leaned against the massive desk in the center of the station. Neither of them looked in my direction. Tammy sighed and sat on the visitor's bench near the door. Oddly, Tammy unfastened the top button of her blouse and leaned back on the bench. In my short time knowing Tammy, I had never seen her present herself in a well put together manner. I felt the frustration of everyone in the room.

"You think Deputy Farley had something to do with Ms. Jones's disappearance? I mean, come on, ma'am… I'll admit he was a bit of an oddball, but a murderer? The kid spent most of his life here in this small town and spent his spare time playing video games. He was about as gentle as they came. Farley wasn't a great deputy, but he didn't show signs of aggression," Sheriff Alfred replied, then turned to Tammy. "Ms. Hodges, is there any chance Ms. Jones was having a depressive episode or—"

"Sheriff, Ms. Jones is as tough as they come and would never disappear like this. She hasn't done anything like this in the ten years I've worked for her. She's smart and tenacious and has too much respect for everything she's built. Why she had a fixation on this town and acquiring as much land here as possible? I'm not sure. As of today, she's the closest she's ever been. Too close to accomplish her goal, so she wouldn't just take off."

As I listened to the words spill past Tammy's lips, it occurred to me that she could have provided the file to Janice anonymously before she died. Tammy worked with her every day and night. If anyone would have known exactly what Ms. Jones' motivations were, it would be Tammy. I knew now wasn't the time to discuss that with her.

"Sheriff, it's not a coincidence that all of this is happening. The missing people, the grotesque deaths of my sister and your deputy, and this witchcraft symbol. Whatever is doing this, it's feeding off the life force of the victims and was conjured by the continuous evil happening here. The cracked gray skin, dehydrated, bloodless bodies, and the ocular void—whatever has awakened, it has an appetite. I hope I'm wrong, but I have a few ideas about what it could be, and none of them are good."

As I stood near everyone in the lobby of the police station, the lights flickered and pulsated as if they were being drained of power. The buzzing sound of pulsating electricity filled the room moments before the spray of shattering lightbulb glass. Everyone ducked in fear with their arms covering their heads. The high-pitched screams of both Tammy and Deputy Shannon echoed from the unexpected shock at the power surge. A piercing, high-pitched wail that followed forced us to cover our ears. I squinted my eyes and clenched my jaw in pain. The crippling, eardrum-splitting sound lasted only a few seconds before the sweet relief of silence once again fell upon the room, leaving behind a slight ringing in my ears. I stood and rushed to the door to identify what could have caused the sound. The others followed as I opened the door and ran outside onto the off-centered wooden porch of the police station. Disoriented and under the darkness of the night sky, I shook my head to ease the discomfort caused by the high-pitched wail.

"I've heard that scream before just a couple of nights ago. It wasn't that loud last time. Whatever it was, it was closer this time than the last," Tammy said. Her hands trembled, and her eyes sat wide with confusion.

A large mahogany-skinned man dressed in a brown trench coat that partially covered his navy-blue suit underneath, stared at the group as we stood on the porch near the station's entrance. "Tammy! Tammy, I've been looking all over this shitty town for you guys. Where the hell have you been? I took a flight as soon as you called and told me what happened. What was that sound?" the man with a baritone voice yelled as he approached the stairs. His eyes lingered on me as I stared back with intrigue.

"Charles, you've made it. We've been waiting—"

Again, the high-pitched wail crippled us as we all fell to our knees and covered our ears. Some of us yelled in pain. The howl was shorter in duration as we all slowly stood once again.

The unexpected appearance of a dark figure caused my eyes to widen at what was standing in the middle of the road, staring back at us. The figure's long, white stringy hair and pupil-less white eyes made the hairs on my arms rise as it glared back at me. It smiled at us with its jagged, sharp teeth.

Its skin appeared coarse and as black as leather, almost blending with the darkness of the night. My stomach turned at the disgusting sight of its thin legs, and knees bent unnaturally in the opposite direction. Its arms were long and thin, and both its feet and hands were three-pronged oversized talons with what looked like viciously sharp claws.

"My God," I mumbled.

Everyone stared at the creature in terror as the claws on its feet waved and tapped against the concrete like fingers of a waiting patron at a bar. It ran away with a bird-like stride in complete silence.

"What the fuck was that, Tammy? And why did it look like my mother?" Charles asked. His voice trembled as he spoke.

Tammy's brow curled. I watched as the tears fell from her eyes.

"T-that face? Yes, Charles. I think it was."

CHAPTER 16

Donald tossed the keys to Sissy. She locked the doors of the diner after re-gaining her bearings from the terrifying wailing screams that she, Jessie, and Donald heard. Nerves rattled, Donald walked around the dining area, looking up at the powerless bulbs from the unexpected loss of electricity. Disoriented, Donald lowered his head, squinted his eyes, and pinched the bridge of his nose. Sissy and Jessie rubbed their temples for what he could only assume was the same headache from the eardrum splitting sound that echoed inside. The darkened interior of the diner, along with its dated aesthetics and worn furniture, helped Donald realize his now darkened environment was just like several of the cheesy horror movies he enjoyed watching. The cheesier the flick, the better, Donald always thought. Only, the thrill of watching from the comfort and safety of his own living room was what made it all a little less terrifying.

"Sissy, that's the third time we've heard that sound. The first time, it wasn't that close. I don't know of any animals that can scream like that. Things are a lot weirder than usual 'round here," Donald said, walking to the front entrance and peering out the window, constantly changing his angle in hopes of a better view of identifying that sound. "Whatever that was, it's not good and I don't think it's a coincidence that it's been around since that night." His raspy voice trembled, and the keys in the door rattled as he turned them back and forth and twisted the handle, struggling to lock the doors of the diner. He hurried and closed the window blinds covered in dust and brownish grease-colored stains.

Donald looked around the diner, frantically pacing and trying to find any last-minute details he might have missed before he and Sissy locked up for the night. A bitter, icy wind rattled the windows and forced the old wooden building to bellow as if the construction struggled to hold itself together.

"Hey guys, since we don't have any lights anyway, I'll clean up a few last things in the kitchen, at least as much as I can before we get out of here. That creepy sound has my nerves bad, plus now I have a terrible headache. It's best if I stay busy till we leave," Jessie said as she finished wiping down the last parts of the counter. "Hey, Uncle Donald, give me the key to the freezer and I can pull all the pork we'll need for tomorrow's batch of stew." Jessie held out her hand and motioned her fingers with anticipation.

"I'll pull the meat for tomorrow after I finish up in here, Jessie. Stop trying to get my goddamn keys all the time, young lady."

Jessie walked through the half-length, double swinging door behind the counter that led to the kitchen.

"Jessie, leave that old sad sack and his freezer alone. Whatever you don't get done tonight, we'll get it done in the morning. I just want to get the hell out of here, sugah," Sissy replied.

The lights flickered as the incandescent bulbs aligned on the ceiling, once again found a steady stream of power.

"Well, praise the Lord. We've got power again. Let's get this place cleaned and locked up, so we can get home to our warm and comfy beds," Sissy said, and smiled at the thought.

Donald cleared the last of the tables. His older frame wasn't as fast as his younger, thinner, twenty-year-old self once was. He often reflected on his high school days and how he wished he could turn the clock back. Full of hope and potential, Donald knew he would end up running someone's corporation one day and not be a hog farmer like his father. Now, that energetic and strong body he once had has faded. The halls of Dalyville High that Donald once strolled as a popular jokester had long been closed. He could have never imagined he would end up still living in his small hometown, running the only diner in town. He had bigger dreams than what he had accomplished, but the love he had for Dalyville wouldn't allow him to leave, even after the soybean farming economy of the town collapsed.

The lights flickered and pulsated again. The incandescent bulbs above shattered as the piercing assault of the wail started. The ear-splitting scream closer than before. Sissy glared at Donald, her eyes wide with concern.

"Goddamnit! I'm not about to let a bunch of screaming and wind run a yellow streak down my back like some coward... After all we've had to do to keep full bellies and a happy home 'round here. I don't think so. Sissy, hand me the shotgun behind the counter," Donald yelled, his face now the color of a bright red candied apple.

"I'll get your damn gun. Just be quiet, you trigger happy fool." Sissy moved as fast as her feet would take her behind the counter.

A high-pitched squeak of a sharp object slowly dragging along the glass came from the front window of the diner. Donald peered through the gaps in the blinds he made with a couple of fingers and saw what appeared to be three large fingernails dragging across. Donald's muscles seized after his sight fell upon the jagged edges of a shadow behind the blinds covering the window near the entrance. Its movement was deliberate, and its jagged features became clearer as it turned its head to look inside. Something walked in plain view of the glass door.

"Don, baby, move away from the window," Sissy pleaded, her voice timid and trembled in fear, recognizably different from only a moment ago.

Donald saw the grotesque creature lift its appendage, place it against the window, and drag it across the glass. The reverberating high-pitched screech caused both Sissy and Donald to flinch and cover their ears, as if it was a fork scraping against a metal surface. Its smile displayed its sharp teeth, while its dead white eyes gazed inside.

Sissy and Donald screamed as they watched the figure stare back at them. Its creepy smile conveyed its hunger. Jessie ducked down behind the kitchen counter, her eyes wide, and her arms wrapped around her tucked knees, cowering from the evil that glared back at her. Its eyes locked on Sissy. The creature placed both clawed hands on each glass door, its jaw opened, and it screamed a high-pitched wail. The glass on both doors shattered; shards of glass covered the ground of the entrance. The snapping sound of its legs as it took steps inside the diner caused Donald to flinch with every step.

Donald stared at its inverted knees and thin frame and ran as best as his older body could manage to protect Sissy. Sissy stood only steps away from the creature. Her attempts to flee as she turned to run caused her to stumble over the legs of one of the dining tables. Her back hit the counter as she barely maintained her footing with her elbows braced on top of the counter. The weight of her heavy frame pulled at her weak arms.

"Oh my God, Donald, look at its face. Look at its face! It's her," Sissy yelled, as she tried to get back on her feet.

"I don't understand. How? You're dead. We killed you."

The creature lunged at both Sissy and Donald as they huddled together, their bodies frozen with fear. Its claws wrapped around the throats of both Donald and Sissy. As it lifted them off the ground, the creature stared at them and slowly lowered its bottom jaw. The cylinder snake shaped tongue slithered out of the creature's mouth and brushed against both Donald's and Sissy's faces. The tip of its tongue opened and closed, baring the pin-like teeth inside it.

Slithering with hunger, the creature slammed its tongue through Sissy's mouth. Her legs struggled to find the ground as she choked. Sissy's body withered as her skin discolored; her eyes turned black, liquified, and poured from their sockets. It released Sissy. A high-pitch cackle of satisfaction followed the thud of her body smacking against the diner's hardwood floors.

Donald tried to scream, but only choked from the squeeze of the creature's claws, as he watched what happened to Sissy. Donald widened his eyes, watching the monster's tongue slither from its mouth again. The smell of its rancid breath forced him to try to turn his head, but he failed to do so. The creature's tongue forced its way into Donald's mouth and latched onto the back of his throat. His body withered and his skin discolored. His eyes liquified into a black sludge and poured down his face. The creature snapped his neck and dropped his body to the floor.

JESSIE SLOWLY RAISED her head from behind the service counter, her breath shaken, and her eyes filled with tears as she peeked over. The horrific sight of the black sludge that poured from her aunt and uncle's empty eye sockets caused her hands to tremble. Her breathing was erratic. The creature smiled at Jessie as it noticed her gaze in its direction. Its grin widened unnaturally, and its dead eyes lingered on Jessie. The creature fled the diner, blowing past tables and tossing them aside as it disappeared into the darkness.

CHAPTER 17

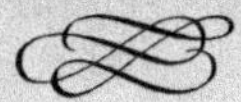

The emergency lighting inside the sheriff's station provided little relief after the assault of the high-pitched wails shattered most of the lightbulbs inside. The dimly lit station was still some relief from the darkness of Main Street and the bitter cold of the winter night's air. An event like that, for the uninitiated into the supernatural world, would usually cause a lot of confusion and fear. I had never seen a group of people calmly walk into a building after such a sight. Hell, even for me, it was the first time I saw anything like that.

Tammy sat on the visitor's bench near the front door with a look of disbelief; her arms rested on her knees and the palms of her hands clutched each side of her head. Sheriff Alfred and Deputy Shannon were visibly shaken as they paced back and forth near each other with ashen faces. The repetitive taps from the heels of their cowboy boots fell into rhythm, while both tapped the handle of their holstered guns, where their hands rested. Typical of a nervous cop. The deputy pulled a cigarette from his top shirt pocket and struggled to light it.

Who in the hell still wears cowboy boots, anyway? I guess the sight of that thing did shake them up a bit.

The door again quickly swung open, and a pale, slender man walked into the sheriff's station. His blue jeans and oversized jacket didn't seem to faze the sheriff or Deputy Shannon. They seemed almost relieved, both with uncomfortable grins on their faces.

"Westin, you're back. It's a hell of a time to come back, and quite a shitstorm to walk into," the sheriff said.

Westin walked in and looked around at the amount of people inside the station, head tilted slightly as he scratched the top of his head in bewilderment.

"Can someone explain to me what the fuck that sound was? I've been back five minutes, and it seems like all hell is breaking loose," Westin said.

I watched as the man the sheriff called Westin walked deeper into the station. His slick black hair and thin nose were familiar in a fresh way.

"Don't I know you?" I asked as I stared at his face.

"No, I don't think so," he replied, looking in another direction.

"Yeah, I think I do know you. Did you enjoy your lunch today?" I asked.

He was familiar from the diner from earlier today, the man who sat closest to the Dalys. He refused to look in my direction. I turned my attention to the other guy standing near Tammy.

The new guy stood near the entrance with his back against the wall, his arms folded, and his brow creased with anger. There was something different about him, though, outside of his visible display of anger—a strength. His posture was that of a career military man. The blue high-end suit that perfectly hugged his muscular frame signaled he was a man that cared about his appearance. He seemed unfazed by the sight of that thing out there, but more shaken by what he thought he recognized about it. He briefly cut his eyes in my direction, squinted, then widened his eyes and relaxed his brow as he stared at me. He quickly turned away.

"Nola, I knew what your sister did and who she worked for. I know about what you both do, and I know about what happened in New Orleans fifteen years ago. I've heard about it, read about it, and talked about it with Janice," Sheriff Alfred said as he walked closer to me, rubbing his hands together nervously. "It's one thing to know about it. It's something completely different to be that close to something like that. What we just saw scared the crap out of me. I've never seen anything like that. What in the hell was that?" the sheriff asked. His voice shook as his words passed his lips.

"Sheriff, I've never seen one before," I said.

"What the hell do you mean? All these years fighting and killing these things and you don't know what it is?"

"I said I've never seen one before. I didn't say I didn't know what it was. I think we have a banshee on our hands." I exhaled sharply.

"Now this is just ridiculous. I've heard enough," Deputy Shannon spewed as he stepped between us and faced Alfred. "Sheriff, you let this woman dick us around on Farley's crime scene, and now she's talking about Irish legends and vengeful spirits. This is a waste of fucking time."

Deputy Shannon had been a pain since the first moment I met him. His arrogant country hick routine had grown tiresome to me quickly.

"Deputy, if you know what we just saw out there, then explain it to us. Did it look human to you?" I asked.

Deputy Shannon stepped closer. I could smell the stench of cigarettes on his breath. His taller, six-foot frame blocked out some of the station's artificial incandescent lighting. Out of my peripheral vision, I saw the sheriff step forward to intervene. I held the palm of my hand out toward him, commanding the sheriff not to come any closer.

"Whatever it was, it could have just as easily been some clown in a fucking costume, running around trying to give you credibility. Or maybe it's some kind of animal or freak wearing a mask? Hell, if you're anything like your uppity sister, it probably wants to kill you, too." His pointed index finger jabbed me in the shoulder.

I've dealt with all manner of creatures. Some of the most beastly and violent agents of evil on this planet, and for the most part, I managed to keep my cool when I hunted. I never found anger to be useful. It blinds you to the situation at hand and often leads to poor judgment, but these past few years were different. My parents' murder and now the murder of Janice had put me in a very different place. The thought of this condescending man's finger violating my personal space put me in a place reserved for only a few of the creatures I've hunted.

A glance at his pointed finger, and I soon realized I had grabbed it, twisted it and his arm over, and elevated it in the air. The sound of the bone in his finger snapping preceded the shrill squeal and distending of his eyes. I lifted my leg and planted a kick to his ribs, sending his body stumbling against the nearby wall and crashing onto the floor. Deputy Shannon grimaced in pain as he rolled onto his hands and knees and struggled to catch his breath.

"C-cuff her, Sheriff. T-that b-bitch is under arrest," Shannon said as he gasped for air.

Deputy Westin's cackling laugh echoed inside as he pointed at Shannon and his pain.

"Settle down, Shannon. We aren't arresting anybody. You put your grimy little hands on her first. You're a good guy, but I always told you that tough guy act was going to lead you right into an ass whoopin' someday. Looks like today was your day," the sheriff said.

"That was pretty impressive, Nola," Tammy interjected as she grinned at the sight of the deputy still gasping for air.

"Shannon, I know you're scared, especially after what we just saw. There is no need to be at each other's throats. We have more pressing things we need to attend to. Like I said, I've never seen one before. They're rare, but I'm pretty sure that was a banshee. The glazed white eyes and the scream fit the profile. If that's the case, however it manifested, it won't stop until it fulfills whatever appetite for vengeance it has," I said.

The faces around the room all just stared back at me as if I was some sort of crazy person screaming on a street corner. All except for one. The gentleman that just came was still focused in thought with his head down and his eyes pointed toward the floor.

"That's not like any banshee I've ever heard of. This is an Irish community, and we're pretty tuned in with our folklore," Sheriff Alfred said as he looked over at the corner of the room and watched Deputy Shannon finally get to his feet.

"Most of the so-called details about the legends you've heard are wrong. Banshees aren't corporal. They aren't bodiless floating entities dressed in all white or black, screaming into the night. Well, the screaming part is right," I said with a slight smirk. "Banshees are vengeful, angry hunters. Their forms vary, but often manifest from the form of the person who could tap into the spiritual energy. The manifestation sometimes happens where the person wronged died. The more spiritual energy at the location where the victim was murdered, the more powerful the banshee. Banshees will kill everything and everyone that was responsible for their death and anyone that stands in their way. Draining their victims' life force and destroying their souls in the process."

"Jesus Christ, it looked just like... I mean, that thing looked like it was built to rip someone apart. The claws and the teeth. I mean, how are we supposed to stop that thing?" Tammy said.

Her eyes glared back and forth between me and the well-dressed stranger near the door.

I'm not sure how I can stop it, I thought.

"Sir, are we disturbing you? What's your name and why are you here?" I already knew the answer. Tammy yelled his name when we were all gathered outside. I needed to get him involved in this conversation.

"His name is Charles. He's the project manager for Ms. Jones. He's also her son." Tammy's voice trailed off at the end.

Charles walked over closer to Tammy and knelt in front of her. I watched as he gently grabbed her shaking hands with care.

"Did you see what I saw, Tammy? Did you see her face?" Charles asked. His baritone voice was smooth and comforting just listening to it.

Charles' thumb gently stroked the top of Tammy's hands as he held it. Tammy's eyes locked on his. There was something deeper there. This wasn't just the prying of information from one person to another or even the concern for a co-worker. This was empathy and possibly even love.

"I saw it Charles," Tammy mumbled. "I saw her. It was her." Her voice cracked as she swallowed, trying to relieve her dry throat.

"I saw it too, Tammy. What in God's name happened here?" Charles asked. His deep voice carried inside the station.

"Saw what, exactly?" I interjected.

Charles stood and walked toward me. Instinctively, I took a step back as he approached. I'm usually not even slightly intimidated by men. I no longer get the butterflies in my stomach or a feeling of attraction to some large burly man in the room. It wasn't that I was no longer attracted to them. I was. I haven't been with a man for quite a while, and I missed the heat and passion that often comes with it. It was just that after fighting and killing the type of beasts I've encountered, everything else takes less of a priority. I decided to focus on the lives I can save doing what I do. I put those potential victims' needs ahead of my own. Then, the incident with my parents happened, and I needed to be strong for the little family I had left. Now, the need to be strong for my family is a reflex. I can't remember the last time being selfish was an option for me. Plus, I still think of James now and then. Not that fucking beast, but James—the smart, sweet, and gentle man I knew before evil consumed him. Somehow, I still felt there was a future for us that was snatched away prematurely.

"That thing out there, it had my mother's face. I've heard of banshee lore. A banshee is a spirit, right? You country hicks haven't found my missing mother yet. She's been missing for three days, and if she looks like that damned thing out there, then she must be dead. It's not wearing her face just for the sport of it." Charles' nostrils flared. "What the fuck have you guys been doing all this time?"

"Look here, son—" the sheriff said gently, stepping toward Charles to put his hand on his shoulder.

"Son?" Charles said in a deliberate tone. He stood quickly and closed the distance between him and the sheriff.

The room fell dead silent, as if some supernatural means had sucked all the oxygen out. "I'm not your son," he whispered, leaning in close to the sheriff's ear, his rather large club-like hands tightly closed.

"Wait one second, it was just a figure of speech. I didn't mean anything by it. I'm not your enemy here. Nola and I have been trying to find your mother and her sister's murderer for the past few days. What you saw tonight was the closest we've been to getting anything that could explain what the hell is going on around here," the sheriff said.

I stepped in between Charles and Sheriff Alfred, a little worn on the display of testosterone, but given the way I treated Deputy Shannon, I'm just as guilty.

"Look, Charles, are you aware of everything that has happened? The supernatural events that have taken place. You seem to have jumped to the conclusion of your mother's death pretty quickly at the sight of that creature," I said.

"I'm aware of some things. I'm not new to what has been happening. My mother's business reaches from New York all the way down to New Orleans. We have ongoing projects there, along with an office. I'm aware of what happened there. I'm down there quite often."

"Well, I'm afraid you're right. If that was a banshee, its spirit manifested and ascended from someone. The timing is right compared to when your mother went missing and when my sister was murdered. Your mother was last seen by Tammy going to the original settlement. One of the last people who saw her—that we know of—was possibly Deputy Farley. Now, he's dead. Something triggered this event that had enough power to turn your mother into this thing, or at least it's using her likeness. We have to figure out what it was and what the hell is going on before more people die."

The door of the sheriff's station pushed open as a hysterical woman made her way in. Her hair was ragged, and her mascara ran down her face as her tears fell. She shook with fear and stuttered as she tried to speak.

"P-Please help. Something happened at the diner. T-they're dead." Jessie barged through the door of the police station, stumbling to her knees. Her body froze in terror, as though she were nailed to the floor of the Dalyville police station.

Moments passed, and she regained the ability to speak. The lack of blood contradicted her rambling tales of unexpected and violent deaths of her bosses at the Dalyville Diner.

"It was the lady, I think. The lady that was here that wanted to build stuff. She looked so horrific. Sheriff, you have to believe me. Aunt Sissy and Uncle Donald are dead. She killed them," Jessie pleaded. She frantically grabbed hold of his arm.

"Sheriff, I don't think our night is over yet," I said, helping Jessie to her feet. "Honestly, I think this creature is just getting started."

CHAPTER 18

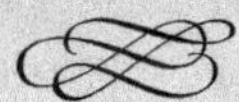

At first glance, the sight of the shattered glass door of the diner and its well lit interior stopped me in my tracks as we approached. The creep factor was bad enough, but it probably wasn't the best idea to bring Jessie and the sheriff back along. If that thing decided it wasn't done here, and showed its hideous face again, I might not be able to protect them. The sheriff may have a gun strapped to his waist, but who the hell knows if he ever had to use that thing when it mattered most. Jessie on the other hand, the way she was gripped in terror when she barged into the sheriff's station it was doubtful her response to the sight of that banshee again would be anything but self-preservation.

I don't know her that well, but I doubt this is an act for attention. Hell, the banshee and its wail was enough to drop the toughest person to their knees.

The dead silence of the post-midnight morning enhanced the discomfort I had from the frigid air and pitch-black void of

Main Street. Even for a small town, it should have done better light maintenance along its main road. I never became comfortable with the dark again after finding out what could lurk within it, but I would never let it compromise what needed to be done. Right now, going through that doorway on a trail of shattered glass was necessary. The attempt to get Jessie to come back here was like a dentist attempting to calm a child before some major procedure. Fear had taken control of her and refused to relinquish its hold, much like her current grip on Sheriff Alfred's arm.

Jessie screamed at the sound of the screeching tires of the braking car behind us. It could rival that of the banshee as it echoed in the night's air. Charles quickly exited out of his car as if a city's police department had trained him to make pedestrian felony stops. There was definitely more to him than being the son of a wealthy real-estate mogul and project manager.

"Is this the place?" Charles stomped toward me. His suit jacket removed, and his bright white, button-down shirt and silk blue tie were still impeccably in place.

"What are you doing here? You should be back at the police station with Tammy and Deputy Shannon. There is no need for you here. Go back and comfort your girlfriend," I insisted.

"Nola, is it? Tammy isn't my girlfriend. She's worked for my mother for a long time, and I've grown to care about her well-being, but we aren't a couple. I'm not her type. Not that I owe you any explanation."

"Apologies, I thought that... The way you were comforting her—"

"We were in love? No. I'm not the Jones that Tammy is in love with. We're just friends, and she trusts me enough to keep her feelings for her boss a secret."

"Oh, I see." I averted my eyes toward the pavement and marveled at my ability to be an asshole these days.

"From what I gather, you're supposed to be some special investigator of all things, including what I would call some fringe incidents. However, don't presume you know me or my capabilities. I'm here for my mother, and if she's dead, I'm going to find out what happened to her, and if I have to, I'll kill the people involved." Charles' voice didn't waver, and his intent was clear. Whatever his background was, he seemed to be confident it would be beneficial to find his mother.

"Okay, Charles. Just stay out of our way and let the sheriff and I do what we're qualified to do," I replied.

"I'm not here to get in your way, Nola. I'm here to find out anything I can about what happened to my mother. If there's anything I can do to save her, I will. If it's too late for that… well, there's not a damn thing anyone here can do to stop me."

I should have been offended, but I wasn't. The confidence with which he spoke was something I hadn't seen in a long time, at least from a human. Vampires always had an overabundance that I found so damn annoying.

"If you two are finished with your pissing contest, can we get going inside?" Sheriff Alfred interjected.

The crackle of the broken glass under my feet served as a makeshift alarm when all four of us entered the diner. Only no one was left alive inside to hear it. The sight of the shriveled gray skin and black sludge dripping from the stiffened bodies caused Jessie to vomit in the corner near the entrance. The fingers on both Donald and Sissy's hands were curled as if they tried to keep a grip on something.

"Damn it. I didn't want to believe it, but that's Donald and Sissy, alright. Jessie, what happened?" The sheriff's voice cracked as he stared down at the bodies. The anger was visible on his tense brow.

"Sheriff, like I said, I was in the kitchen finishing up some last-minute cleaning. Sissy and Donald were up front talking." Jessie paused as she covered her mouth and turned away from the sight of the bodies. Her breathing was erratic as she pushed through the nausea to speak. "T-then we heard the scream, and that thing was at the front door, staring at them. It just stood there with a creepy grin and its dead white eyes. Its claws pressed up against the glass of the door as it cracked and eventually shattered the glass," Jessie said.

"I don't understand, Nola. You said that banshees are born from and driven by vengeance. These people never bothered no one. I've known them since I was a kid. I mean, Sissy was one of the sweetest persons I knew," Sheriff Alfred said; his voice cracked again.

"Alfred, if that thing was after them—" I started. Jessie exhaled heavily and stood up as she gathered herself.

"Sheriff, I thought so too. Auntie Sissy and Uncle Donald were always so nice. Especially after my parents died. They were nothing like cousin Jerry and cousin Jean. At least, I didn't think so," Jessie interrupted. She stood in front of the sheriff; her head turned, looking down at the bodies. "I could hear them yell from the kitchen. They recognized it. I recognized it. I heard them both scream, 'you're dead.' Ms. Nola, it was that lady—the rich one from New York. Last I heard, she was missing, and no one found her yet."

"That's right. Ms. Jones is still considered missing," I replied.

"That's what I thought. I'm not sure what happened, but after I heard them say that, I remembered how they closed the diner early a couple of nights ago. Uncle Donald and Auntie Sissy never closed early. I didn't question it too much because I could use the extra time off."

"What reason did they give for the early closure?" I asked.

"They mentioned something about a party with our cousins, the other Dalys. I didn't think much of it since it was family and cousin Jerry is the mayor, but two nights ago, that's when that lady went missing, isn't it?" Jessie asked.

The sheriff pulled a chair from under a nearby table and fell into it. His head planted firmly into the palm of his hands.

"What in the hell is going on in my town? Who are these people?" the sheriff mumbled. "I refuse to believe they would be involved with something like that."

"They were kind people, Sheriff. They were always sweet to me, great bosses too, but—" Jessie paused, lowering her head.

"But, what, Jessie?" I pressed.

"But I sometimes heard them whisper. They sometimes whispered some horrible things about outsiders or people different from us," Jessie mumbled. Her shoulders shifted away from the corpse as her head lowered once again. "They liked to keep secrets. Hell, Uncle Donald kept most of his food recipes locked in cabinets or locked in the freezer, with the only key in his possession. So, no one can rip off his recipes, as Donald often put it."

Sheriff Alfred stood over his once lively and funny friends. He reached for his radio clipped to his shoulder; his lip folded in as he exhaled sharply. The crackle of the radio was intrusive as his thumb prompted the receiver.

"Shannon, are you there? Come in."

"I'm here, Sheriff."

"Look, go ahead and wake up the coroner, and get him out here as fast as possible. That thing killed Donald and Sissy. We want to clean this up before sunrise when townsfolk start coming around. I'll drop Jessie off at home. I want you to take Tammy back to her motel. We'll pick this all up in the morning and I'll get Reggie to board up this place," the sheriff ordered.

"My God. 10-4, Sheriff," Deputy Shannon replied.

"Sheriff, tomorrow I'm going to look into the Dalys and see what happened that night. Whatever they know or whatever they did could be key to gaining an advantage in stopping this thing, or at the minimum, get us some understanding of what could've happened." I locked eyes with Jessie.

The sight of Jessie's tears caused me to lose focus as I thought about the family I lost. My hands began to shake, and I quickly shoved them in my coat pockets to hide them. One thought consumed me as I stared at Jessie.

My sister is gone, and there is nothing I can do to bring her back.

"Nola. Nola! You hear me?" Sheriff Alfred yelled, waving his hand in front of my face. I shifted my eyes toward him.

"Do you have anything else you want to look at here?"

"Not tonight, Sheriff. This will all be here in the morning. Once the coroner picks up the bodies and the diner is boarded up, I'll come back and look around a little more. I'm headed home. Charles, I advise you to get a room where Tammy is staying. I'll find you tomorrow," I said.

"We're not done here. At the least, we can search the town for it while we're out here. This place isn't that big," Charles insisted.

"We're done for the night. I'm sure Sheriff Alfred agrees with me. I'm not sure who you think you are, but maybe you should spend some time with Tammy. Your friend needs you right now, and you need her. I know the pain and uncertainty you are feeling right now and that it's your mother out there. Still, running around in the freezing darkness of night is pretty damn stupid, Charles."

Charles stared back at me. His face was still. There wasn't a look of anger, contempt, or even frustration. He just stared back at me and curled his lips inward, as if he was choking back words he desperately wanted to sling in my direction.

"I'll do it your way... tonight, and only for tonight," Charles replied.

"Charles, I promise you, we'll find out what happened to your mother and my sister."

"You'll see me tomorrow, Nola. Count on it."

I hurried back to the car, my head spinning from the day's events, trying to establish an understanding of what happened here. My thoughts returned to the death of Janice by this creature, hands still shaking as I placed them on the steering wheel.

Ms. Jones was hunted and killed. The question is what parties were involved. How did she become a banshee?

"This will get bloodier."

CHAPTER 19

It had been years since I felt the safety and comfort provided by any set of walls and a ceiling. Yet, somehow when I walked into the home made by Janice and Darrius, something nurtured from the moment they stepped inside, I felt it. I felt the safety and comfort I longed for so often after all these years. Even with all that was going on, the small sense of relief I had when I walked through those doors had to be enough for now. Right now, the only thing that mattered was figuring out what exactly happened to Ms. Jones and how many more bodies will this thing claim.

The rapid thump of footsteps that came from behind me accompanied the crackle of the splintering wood in the fireplace. The sight of Jackson and his look of worry were what I expected after abandoning him for most of the day. Juxtaposed with the sight of Darrius stumbling through the adjacent hallway, still inebriated. This angered me to the point where I wasn't opposed to giving him a much-needed punch in the face to knock some sense into him, or, if for no other reason than to sober him up. Now wasn't the time to point out his current failures as a father.

"Don't look at me like that. You're the last person who should look at me with judgmental eyes. You probably have a bottle of vodka stashed somewhere in that bedroom of yours," Darrius said.

"Darrius, I haven't had a drink since I've been in town. My priority is to take care of you two and find my sister's killer. It'd be helpful if you did the same."

Darrius straightened his stance and glared at me with contempt. His eyes wavered in Jackson's direction as his tense brow softened at the sight of him.

"I'm sorry, son. I haven't been there like I should be. The pain has been overbearing. I know that's no excuse. You've felt the same pain I have." Darrius' head lowered as he mumbled.

"Boys, I hate to interrupt this moment, but I came with some news. I think I know what killed Janice," I said.

After the words passed my lips, regret pooled in the pit of my stomach. Darrius and Jackson needed that time to talk and work through their pain. They deserved that time. Time, I didn't have, and time better served doing the job.

"You've heard the wailings the past few nights. Well, there have been three more people murdered in the exact same way as Janice. It appears it's a banshee."

"A banshee? Why the hell would a banshee want to kill Mom?"

"I don't think it wanted to kill her, Jackson. I think the timing of her being at the settlement was bad, really bad. It's my theory that Janice was the first person it saw when it manifested, and I believe I already know who the banshee could be. The whys and the hows are what's needed before I can figure out a way to kill it," I said.

"You said you know the person who caused the manifestation of the banshee? Was it in that file that showed up at the door?" Darrius asked.

I turned and faced Darrius. He stood there with his arm above his head braced up against the wall, supporting his weight. Tears fell from his eyes as he awaited an answer. His vulnerability was something I had never seen in Darrius in all the years I'd known him.

"Yes. I didn't tell the others about the file yet, but someone dropped it off here. My bet is it was Tammy, Ms. Jones's assistant, probably at the request of Ms. Jones. From what I gathered, certain facets of the town didn't like Ms. Ashley Jones or her plans for the future here. Apparently, there was some sort of scheme planned the night she went missing. It also looks as though the Dalys were involved somehow. I plan on nailing down what's going on tomorrow with the sheriff," I said. I turned away from Darrius and moved a little closer to Jackson. "I have an impression I took earlier at the settlement, but I need to investigate a little deeper. Do you wanna give me a hand?"

"Hell yes!" Jackson replied with a smile and an expression of genuine happiness that momentarily pushed through.

As we stepped foot back into Janice's office, I was reminded how different our focus was when it came to investigations. We both knew the different lore of most of the creatures out there. It was Janice's insistence on knowing the history that separated us. Janice not only wanted to know the strengths and weaknesses of every creature we encountered, but the origins and history as well. Janice had an excitement about her when she researched. Watching Jackson beam with delight in his eyes, I could only assume he shared that enthusiasm for knowing the entire picture, just like his mother.

"Where do you want to start, Auntie?" Jackson asked from behind his mother's desk.

"Okay, let's see what you're made of, nephew." I pulled the small notebook I used at the well from my pocket. "I sketched this impression when I inspected the well at the settlement. They were carved on the inside wall. I'm sure this is witchcraft, but the specifics are a little unfamiliar."

Jackson unfolded the impression, and a smile slowly crept onto his face. His smile could brighten even this dimly lit room. He jumped up from the chair and retrieved a makeshift book from the shelf. The paper seemed tarnished and brittle; and it was bound by a few threads of thin rope intertwined through the pages and flimsy leather material for the cover. He sat back down and added a quick spin in the chair before he opened the book and flipped through the pages as if it was a newly minted textbook from school.

"I've seen that symbol before," Jackson said, flicking through the book in search of the right page. "Yeah, here we go. Mama told me every book in this room would be useful one day. This is a book she put together of witchcraft symbols used in different hunts she had through the years. That symbol is called a Witches Knot. As you can see, it has four interlocking vesica piscis shapes pointing in each of the cardinal directions: north, south, east, and west. Sometimes with a center drawn with a central circle. This carving doesn't have one."

Jackson spun the book around and held up the page, so I could see it. I narrowed my eyes and leaned forward.

"Anyway, it's a symbol of protection, often used as a love charm. It can symbolize the love shared between two or more people. There are a lot of different knots, but this one is the most common," Jackson lectured. The smirk on his face was a full display of pride in his knowledge.

"I have to say, Jackson, your mom taught you well. The carvings in the well were smooth and narrow. It's hard to decipher from the impression, but the knot was definitely carved with a sharp object and smoothed out a little with something coarse. If I had to guess, the person who did it was obviously a practicing witch. The fact that the carvings had brush marks to smooth it out means they must have used hag stone," I explained, tapping the impression with my finger as it lay on the desk. "Are you familiar with it?"

"I've heard of it, but I'm not sure what it's for," Jackson said.

"It's used to ward off witches, but if a witch used it, it was to strengthen the magic against the effects of running water. Running water dampens magic, but if the witch was powerful enough, the hag stone could be used to hide her magic against those that might know some sort of witchcraft was used in the area. The early settlers' daughter, Fiadh Daly, was my suspicion," I replied.

I couldn't help but smile at Jackson's confidence and his eagerness. Janice and Darrius did a great job of raising him. Jackson seemed prepared and possessed the tools he needed to protect himself in an unforgiving world.

"This is what I don't understand, Auntie, given what my mom taught me about this town. Why would a white Irish witch take the chance of carving a symbol into the interior of a well over an enslaved girl in the middle of the settlement? Do you think they really loved each other?"

"I'm sure they loved each other, Jackson. The chances they took during that time… It must have been terrifying. So, we have a young couple with a forbidden love on so many social levels. After she killed her enslavers, Hannah ran, was captured, then lynched, and dumped in this godforsaken well with the bodies of her deceased tormenters. That's a hell of a lot of vengeful energy concentrated in the same place. The carved symbol made that well almost sacred. That symbol was a binding spell. It only makes sense that all that pain and blood turned the spell bad."

"Auntie, just looking at the carving, a witch wouldn't take the time to use hag stone to smooth it out if it wasn't carved with something special, or if they wanted to make the binding as strong as possible. Most of the older witches used an athame, which is a type of dagger. Maybe Fiadh had some old-world ways."

"Jackson, when they came here, it was old world, kiddo," I said with laughter. "You bring up an interesting point, though. What if it wasn't a spell? If both of the young girls were involved with putting it there, it could have been more of a tribute to mother earth than some sort of binding spell. Either way, it's still energy, and the dumping of three bodies where it was carved isn't good. Especially if one of those bodies was a part of the bind there originally," I said.

The thunderous sound of a slamming door startled me. Both Jackson and I ran to the front of the house to a still empty room, only burdened by the crackle of the burning wood in the fireplace. A car engine starting outside forced me toward the door.

"Stay here, Jackson."

I ran out the front door to the sight of Darrius speeding off. The red lights of his vehicle faded in the night as he sped away, driving in the direction of the settlement.

"Son of a bitch."

~

THE VIOLENT BOUNCING FRAME OF DARRIUS' speeding car ripped through the grass of the settlement. The tires kicked up dirt as the tail end of the car swerved from side to side before it came to a sliding stop. Steam rose from under the hood, hissing in the darkness of night as if the engine were infested with snakes. Darrius opened the car door and fell out onto the ground. A bottle half filled with whiskey followed immediately after.

Darrius leveraged the car door and staggered to his feet, with his breathing labored.

"Where the fuck are you?" The sound of his scream echoed off the century old buildings. "I'll search every one of these fucking shacks and find you. You took something from me and... and I'm going to kill you for it." His voice cracked as the words he spewed echoed in the darkness.

The frigid night air had a sobering effect on Darrius as he looked around at the crescent-shaped layout of the buildings. The well that he overheard Nola and Jackson talking about sat in the center of it all. Everything was already difficult to see in the poorly lit area, but his tear filled eyes made it almost impossible to see clearly. Darrius screamed and threw the bottle in the well's direction, shattering it against the brick frame.

"Where are you, goddamn it?"

Darrius walked to the first wooden structure on his left. He retrieved his phone from his back pocket. He squinted at the brightly illuminated screen as he searched for the flashlight app. The stairs squeaked under his weight as he climbed and approached the weatherworn front door. As he wrapped his fingers around the doorknob, he pulled his hand back and shook it. He grimaced in pain.

"Damn it! Real smart, Darrius. Freezing temperatures and a brass doorknob, that'll sober you up." He wrapped his hand with the bottom of his shirt and opened the door.

The cabin was dank and smelled of molded wood and rotten food left from disrespectful partiers. The craftsmanship held up particularly well, but it still felt as if it was a portal into some cruel past. Darrius pulled a semiautomatic handgun from his waistband and held his phone flashlight up in front of him with the other. As often as he thought about the inside of these settlement houses, it didn't quite meet his expectations. The thought was that the town probably had some of the original furniture inside and had the place staged like a museum. Instead, inside was littered with candy wrappers and empty cans of beer, most likely from the exploits of a few rambunctious youths that wandered here from Nashville, chasing ghost tales.

The age of the floorboards caused them to moan under Darrius' weight. The lone window in the first room looked out to a much smaller shed-like home in the rear, with only one door and one window. The sight of the small slave cabin caused Darrius to shift his shoulders uncomfortably, knowing exactly what it was when he saw it.

"I know you're in here. I figured this would be the one your coward ass would hide in. It was theirs, the First Family. I figure evil prefers the company of evil, right?" Darrius yelled out. "Why did you do it? Why did you have to kill Janice?"

As he made his way to the second room, the still quiet and stale air made him shift his shoulders again. The unusual thing about his discomfort was that he wasn't until this moment. What was also unusual was the lack of dust and empty beer cans like the previous room. It didn't make any sense. Why would a bunch of kids keep one room spotless while leaving the other a makeshift garbage can? Darrius' breathing became labored at the suddenly thick air. The only thing that remained in this particular room was the brick-built fireplace filled with centuries old soot.

"Fucking empty," Darrius grumbled, exhaling sharply.

His hands began to tremble. The rattling plastic against the metal of the semiautomatic handgun became thunderously loud in his head.

"Where are you goddamnit?" he yelled, erratically firing several shots into the floor and walls surrounding him.

Shards of splintered wood jumped from the floor and walls as the bullets tore through the structure. Tears fell from Darrius' eyes at the thought of his wife.

The damage gave Darrius little satisfaction. The minuscule sized holes weren't as large as he thought they would be when he removed the gun from the case in Janice's office. Except for one particular area. In the far corner of the room, a hole the size of a softball was in the floor. Darrius' brow furrowed at the sight of the hole and the dust that erupted from underneath the floor. He moved closer and squinted his eyes, lowering himself to one knee trying to see below. The subtle brush of wind against his face caused him to fall back onto his back and push himself away with the heels of his feet. Both the phone and gun slipped from his grasp. Darrius knew the amount of wind coming from underneath a building that sat maybe two feet off the ground made no sense unless there was some sort of storm. The night was cold, but it was clear.

He stood and picked up his phone and gun in his hand, then stomped toward the hole. Darrius lifted his knee and repeatedly stomped on the old, yet still sturdy, wooden floor until his knees and feet ached. He shot several more rounds near the hole and watched as the particles of wood fell below. Darrius kept stomping until large splinters of wood fell beneath, leaving only a narrow square hole. As he peered below, the darkness obstructed his vision and only left the partial vision of several rectangularly cut wood pieces nailed to the interior wall.

"What in the hell?"

Darrius once again kneeled, trying to shine the flashlight below to see the bottom of what appeared to be some sort of tunnel. He placed the gun on the floor beside him and slowly reached his hand inside. With the base of his hand, Darrius pushed on the first plank of wood nailed to the wall to test its strength. The light from the cell phone provided little help to see below.

Christ, I'd do better having some kids' night-light. This has to be pretty deep.

The uneasy feeling in his stomach provided a significant amount of doubt about whether he should descend. Darrius lay on his stomach and again slowly stuck his arm into the hole. He hung his head slightly over the edge, hoping to get some idea of how deep the hole went.

Tunnel? Is it a tunnel? Why would those old farmers dig this creepy hole?

He stood and shook his head at what he was about to do.

My wife would go down there without a second thought. All those years of watching you do the impossible, Janice, it must have rubbed off on me.

As he turned to lower his foot inside, a woman's voice caused him to hesitate. He turned again, unsuccessfully illuminating anything below with the flashlight.

"Hello?" Darrius yelled as he peeked down hastily.

The piercing sound of the scream he heard several times before caused him to instinctively place his hands over his ears, still clutching both the gun and cell phone. The head-splitting scream disoriented him, then it abruptly stopped. This time, the sound was closer than it had been before. Darrius' head thumped with pain while he tried to look inside again. He screamed in terror. A contorted, face with sharp, jagged teeth looked back at him, slightly covered in darkness. Darrius dropped his cell phone and tightly gripped the gun with both hands.

The elongated claws reached up from both sides of the hole. Its sharp edges penetrated the wood as it pulled up its slender body. It screamed as several more rounds fired by Darrius ripped through its torso. The creature's jaw opened wide enough to consume any small animal it could sink its teeth into. It again let out a nerve-rattling scream as it sank its three-pronged clawed feet into the wooden floor, tearing through it as if it was nothing but paper.

Darrius frantically pulled at the trigger of his gun. The sounds of repeated clicks were the only thing it produced. He turned and ran toward the door. His legs lagged behind the orders given to them by his brain. The banshee lunged at Darrius from behind and ripped his flesh along the entirety of his back. He grabbed onto the wall to stay on his feet and screamed in agony, attempting to make his way to the front door. His attempt failed. The banshee again tore through his flesh. Warm fluid gushed and poured down his spine.

He stumbled onto the cold wood of the porch. Sharp pains shot through his knees and elbows as he frantically tried to crawl away. The creature's claws tapped against the wood, trailing behind him. Darrius tumbled down the stairs and back onto his hands and knees, weakened from the loss of blood. The sight of oncoming car headlights helped him to focus and provided him with some hope. He reached out toward the light and attempted to scream, but only blood spewed from his mouth. The darkness of the night became darker as he collapsed onto the grass. His eyes closed forever.

CHAPTER 20

Sheriff Alfred and Deputy Westin pulled up in front of the prodigious home of the first family of Dalyville. The brightness of the morning sun shimmered off the teal color of the house. It looked as though it could be the model dream home of millions of suburbanites just about anywhere in America, at least the size of it, not so much its decor. The sight of the home always struck the sheriff in the wrong way. Dalyville was on life support, and the mayor and his wife did little to fix it. As a matter of fact, Mayor Jerry Daly always seemed more interested in keeping things exactly the way they had always been. Except they weren't the same. The farms had failed. There were no factories. Most of the tax revenue came from visiting college kids who wanted a firsthand look at the so-called haunted settlement or weekend binge drinking parties without law enforcement interference. The mayor made sure of that for reasons unknown to the sheriff.

Still, to see such a lavish home, at least by Dalyville standards, in the middle of a mostly worn and dated town, felt irresponsible at the least. It appeared to mock the few residents that remained. Unfortunately, the townspeople ignored it, mostly. After all, it's the Mayor of Dalyville. The descendent of the founders. They're good, wholesome, red-blooded Americans. A frequent argument from others, even from the sheriff's own deputies when he brought up equipment issues or structural problems at the station. It wasn't until recent events that made the sheriff look a little deeper and questioned what in the hell was going on in his town.

"Westin, we're only going here to ask a few questions. You know how sensitive they can get when someone questions them...for any reason," Sheriff Alfred warned.

"Honestly, Sheriff, I don't know what we're doing here at all. I mean, what would Mr. and Mrs. Daly know about the disappearance of some outsiders?"

"All avenues of any investigation need to be followed up. I have a witness that stated the Dalys might have seen Ms. Jones the night she disappeared. We have to follow up on that deputy. You've been around long enough to know how this works. Small town or not, I don't care how I got this job. I understand I only won the election for sheriff because the Dalys endorsed me. None of that matters. They elected me to do a job, and I'm going to do it."

"I get that, but do you think it's wise to knock on the mayor's door and interrogate him?" Deputy Westin asked. His jaw tensed as he stared at Sheriff Alfred.

"There is no interrogation. We're here to ask him and the missus a few questions. Besides, don't you think Mayor Daly would want to help find any person that comes up missing in his town? I'm sure we'll be in and out before you know it." Sheriff Alfred stared back at his deputy and watched as he shifted in his seat.

"Yeah, but why now? Others have disappeared."

"Westin, others have disappeared, but they weren't verified to have ever visited. That's the difference. A big difference" Sheriff Alfred twisted in his seat trying to square his shoulders toward Westin. "I don't like your attitude right now. You put that badge on to serve this community. I don't need someone who's gonna be a coward when it comes to questioning a small-town mayor. If something like this gets your panties in a bunch, what happens if some shit really went down, and I need you to have my back?"

Deputy Westin, like himself, was born here and probably looked up to the Dalys and their history. The small-town label was a badge of honor. It wasn't as if he never left his little slice of America before, but it was more likely than not that the biggest city he'd ever been to was just a short ride north to Nashville, Tennessee. Still, Alfred couldn't appreciate how intimidating this could be for Westin.

The officers exited the police cruiser and made their way up the stairs of the ranch style home. The bright teal color outside clashed with the deep mahogany tone of the wrap-around porch, which easily snaked its way around three-fourths of the house. Mrs. Daly accented most of it with oversized potted rubber plants, but left special consideration for the TV tray tables and old-fashioned rocking chairs for the front end. It was as though they were trying to make two statements that clashed with each other in a spectacular way. *Look at us, we're very important, and look at us, we're simple, down-to-earth people.* It was a little too much for the sheriff's liking.

The sheriff knocked on the door as politely as he could, still loud enough that someone would know there were visitors outside. There was no response from within. Sheriff Alfred darted his eyes to the driveway and noticed the mayor's pick-up truck parked on the side.

Somebody's home.

He hesitated to knock harder to ensure someone inside heard. Still, both the sheriff and the deputy stood on opposite sides of the thick wooden door, in front of the body-length, designer-stained windows on each side. The windows had assorted bright colors and were insulting to his eyes. Sheriff Alfred peered inside as he placed his forehead against the glass; both hands cupped on the side of his face shading his eyes.

"You know, I've always found it a bit weird, Westin."

"What's that, Sheriff?"

"This is a pretty decent sized house. Looks like lots of rooms inside. Why wouldn't they bother to put in a doorbell, but instead installed a security camera right above the door?"

The sheriff and the deputy peered up and looked directly at the camera above.

"How can we help you, Paul?" the voice on the other end asked.

"Mr. Mayor, I... I wanted to talk to you if you didn't mind." The sheriff squinted his eyes to get a better view inside. His voice trembled a little as he thought about the mayor's ability to crush his re-election campaign.

"Questions about what, Paul? We aren't really in the mood for visitors today."

"This would be easier if you came outside or let us in, but have it your way, sir. We're here to ask a few questions about Ms. Ashley Jones. You know, the outsider buying up all the land? She's been missing for a few days."

The silence on the other end of the door was there for more than what would be considered an uncomfortable amount of time. Sheriff Alfred and Deputy Westin glanced in each other's direction. Sheriff Alfred instinctively placed his hand on his holstered handgun as the silence prolonged.

"Mayor Daly, are you there, sir? We have a little bit of a lead on where Ms. Jones was seen last, and I think you could help us," Sheriff Alfred said. His voice was back in his authoritative tone. The continued silence on the other side of the door caused him to go from feeling uncomfortable, to downright guarded. His hand gripped the handle of his gun and his knuckles turned pale from the squeeze.

"Sheriff, I'm going to say this one time, if you want to get re-elected, you should leave, now. I'm not interested in what you have to ask me or what you have to say. This is my town, and it will stay my town," Mayor Daly spewed.

Sheriff Alfred noticed Deputy Westin's glare as he awaited his response. Westin raised his eyebrows as high as he could manage to get them; his mouth slightly open as he appeared uncomfortable with the direction of the conversation.

"Sir, it's just a couple of questions, and you might be able to save someone's life. I've learned how you feel about...Let's just call them outsiders. These are still people, Mr. Mayor. You could help save a life," the sheriff pleaded.

"We don't give a shit about her life. She's trying to buy up our town and turn it into some goddamn liberal utopia. It's best you leave. Now!"

"Jobs, sir. It's just jobs."

"What the hell did you just say to me?" The mayor's tone climbed a couple of octaves higher.

"Sir, you need to step outside—"

The thunderous sound from inside was quickly followed by the shattering of the glass window near the door. Shards of glass sliced up the sheriff's face. The buckshot ripped through his chest and pushed the sheriff down the stairs and onto his back. His blood poured from his chest and stomach onto the frigid concrete; his eyes still wide from the shock. His life extinguished.

"Holy fuck, he went down like a sack of potatoes." Deputy Westin laughed. The sound of his obnoxious cackle easily passed through the shattered window and filled inside the Dalys home.

"Westin, will you shut the fuck up? Drag the body to the back of the house before somebody drives by and sees him," Mayor Daly yelled, stepping out the front door with a shotgun clutched near his chest. "This motherfucker caused me to damage a perfectly good, designer, stained-glass window. This will be a pain in the ass to replace." He stomped his foot on the wooden porch.

Mayor Daly relaxed his grip on the shotgun and let it dangle from his hand as he watched the deputy drag the sheriff's body toward the rear of the house. He smiled at the appearance of the streaks of blood along the walkway.

"I was getting real tired of him anyway. Get that piece of shit to the back, and bury him deep. Make sure to give my wife's flower bed all the fertilizer it needs in the soil," Mayor Daly said. "His dumb ass should have known better."

CHAPTER 21

The sight of the freshly frosted over grass, sunkissed by the dawn of a new day, clashed with the dark crimson flow of blood that still spilled from Darrius' back. I wiped away the only tear I could manage as I stared at his lifeless body laying cold upon the ground. My body shivered from the cold. I clenched my jaw and inhaled deeply. I felt numb. Unable to process what exactly I saw. What was clear to me was that I let another family member down. As I stood next to Jackson, I found myself in the same position I had been in since the murder of my parents, if I broke down, I wouldn't be any good to anyone.

Especially now. Right now, Jackson needs me.

Jackson knelt beside Darrius. His tears fell, and he bellowed in pain at the sight of his father. His cries echoed in the crescent shaped field. I knelt down beside him and wrapped my arms around his shoulders as tightly as I could. The sound of Jackson's sobs sent a chill down my back that followed with a gut-wrenching pain, while I listened to him call out for his father. His pain was familiar. The loss of a mother and a father at the hands of something born from the darkness would leave a permanent void within. Especially if he felt their deaths were avoidable. I knew they were.

"You stupid son of a bitch, Darrius. Why did you come out here? Why did you come after it alone?" I mumbled. I had to find a way to kill that damn banshee. It took Jackson's mother and father—and my sister. "Jackson, sweetheart... Jackson, I need you to get up. Listen to me." I turned his head to face me. "I need you to go to the car and get a couple of flashlights, Corbin, and my shoulder holster out of the trunk of the car. I'll call the sheriff, so he can get the coroner out here and get your father."

Jackson jerked away and turned his head back toward his father. His cries continued, as he pounded the frozen ground with his fist.

"I need you to try to focus. Go to the car and get my things, so we can clear this cabin. The banshee must be nearby." I turned his head back toward me. Breaking wasn't an option I wanted for Jackson, not with that monster still out here. I had to get him to focus on something else, at least for a while.

Why don't you look like the rest of the victims, Darrius? I studied his body briefly. I couldn't stand to look at Darrius for long, not in that condition.

As Jackson continued to sob, he stood and jogged off to the car. I pulled out my phone and dialed the sheriff. After I made my way up the stairs of the settlement house, I tried to peek inside the doorway, the sight of Darrius' blood along the wooden floor caused my heart to sink a little further. The phone rang on the other end. Its continuous, evenly spaced tones only managed to annoy me as it buzzed in my ear. As I peered through the window, the sight of Darrius' blood on the floor caused my stomach to turn. He was as close to a brother as I had.

"Auntie Nola, h-here you go." Jackson handed me Corbin and a flashlight.

I slid on the shoulder holster and secured Corbin.

"Sheriff isn't answering his phone. I'll try again a little later, but right now, Jackson, we have to clear this shack. We need to find out what your father found in here."

"What do you mean?" Jackson asked. His breathing was erratic as he wiped his tears away with his shirtsleeve.

"Your mama took care of you. She trained you. Focus. I need you to come with me, and I need you to have my back inside. Whatever the reason your dad went inside, that thing chased him back out. That means it was protecting something close by, and that means there is something in the area that probably connects to it." I placed my hand on his shoulder and gently massaged it. Jackson's body trembled and his lip quivered as his eyes darted back at his father. My eyes welled, and a tear fell down my cheek. I pushed down the urge to cry and I quickly wiped it away. "You coming in here with me goes against everything I believe in, but I can't leave you out here by yourself. Every one of the deaths that happened has been at night. I'm beginning to believe that is the only time it hunts, but I'm not one hundred percent on that theory. So, I need you to stay behind me. You are not to engage with anything we find in here. I just need a second set of eyes. If there is any danger or that thing shows up, I want you to run like hell. Don't worry about me; just run. Do you understand, Jackson?"

"B-but I could—"

"No! Do you understand?"

Jackson exhaled and shook his head timidly. Tears continued to fall from his eyes as he cut his eyes over toward his father's body again. "I understand."

As I walked through the front doorway, there was plenty of light from the daylight that leaked inside. Although the old and fractured wood allowed for the light to leak in, it also seemed to do an unexpectedly effective job at not only letting in the cold frigid air, but keeping the air inside as well. Somehow, it was colder inside the cabin than it was outside in the open area of the settlement. My heated breath released a small cloud when I exhaled. Unfortunately, the unexpected rush of chasing behind Darrius in the early morning hours left me wearing only a thin white shirt and gray sweatpants. Perfect for lounging near the warmth of my sister's fireplace, but not much use as tactical gear or protection in these freezing temperatures.

"Jackson, stay close and pay attention to detail. We need to find out what happened, but we may have to move fast to get the hell out of here."

"I've heard about this. When those college kids from Nashville come to town, they used to sneak out here and party," Jackson said somberly, his voice shaky.

The spatter of Darrius' blood along the floor and walls made it difficult to focus. Tiny bumps covered my skin as the frigid air assaulted my body through the thin clothing. The loud clank of an empty beer can shattered the deafening silence as it bounced against the nearby wall. I glared at Jackson in disbelief as I placed my finger on my lips and widened my eyes.

"Shhh, watch your feet," I whispered.

I grabbed the onyx-colored handle of Corbin and pulled it from my shoulder holster, pointing it ahead and slightly tilted down. The years of searching dark abandoned buildings from my time as a detective to chasing all types of creatures over the years didn't make these building searches any easier. Every time was like the first time. I always thought that was a good thing. The moment you start to just go through the motions would most likely be the moment your hunt ends.

"Auntie, look." Jackson pointed from behind me. His trembling hand extended past the side of my face.

I entered the doorway of the room ahead. It was much of the same, except for the smaller brick enforced fireplace on the far side, and the spattered array of bullet holes in the floor and walls.

"Jesus, Darrius, you really did a number on this place."

I widened my eyes at the sight of Jackson standing near the square hole in the floor in the far corner of the room. The depth of its darkness rivaled the pitch black of that night fifteen years ago behind the levee wall in New Orleans. I needed light then, and having some now wouldn't be a bad idea.

"You see that?" Jackson once again pointed his finger.

"Yeah. It looks like some sort of makeshift ladder built into the wall below."

"What do you think is down there, Auntie?" Jackson said, his voice a little steadier.

"Not sure, but I need to do this myself. Stay here, Jackson, and yell if you see anything out of the ordinary. I mean, anything," I said, placing my hand on Jackson's shoulder.

"No problem, Auntie. I can take care of myself." Jackson bent over and reached down, pulling out a large, serrated hunting knife from an ankle holster. "Silver, just in case," he whispered. "Just like Mama taught me." Jackson's eyes welled again.

Seeing Jackson's teary eyes at the mention of Janice made it feel as if I had a lump in my throat. His eyes the color of red flames from the tears that had recently fallen for his murdered father. Janice's tendency to prepare accordingly was a trait my nephew obviously learned from her. I holstered Corbin and placed the butt end of the mini flashlight in my mouth, slowly descending the old makeshift ladder. The darkness thickened the deeper I climbed. The illumination from the flashlight couldn't reach the bottom, but it did an adequate job of showing me the disgusting layers of webs and the hand-sized spiders crawling along the walls that called it home. The longer I climbed down, the more the depths of the darkness seemed never-ending.

I've killed werewolves, vampires, wraiths, and all types of beasts, but the sight of these damn spiders is making me tremble like a bitch. Get it together, Nola.

The trickling sound of water below me approached fast when my feet unexpectedly touched the jagged rock bottom floor. The area was a tunnel that was barely high enough for me to stand. Behind me was a makeshift stone wall stacked with rather large rectangular stones and covered with the green sludge of algae. The miniature stone wall appeared old yet sturdy; it had a small gap at the base where water seeped through and moistened the ground underneath. On the far end of the other side of the tunnel, a faint but natural light was present.

"Auntie Nola, are you okay?" The echo of Jackson's voice barely reached down.

"I'm fine. There seems to be some sort of tunnel. Stay there. I'm going to walk it and see what I can find."

As I trudged through the blackness of the underground tunnel, the dank smell of moistened earth and constant barrage of spiderwebs, the light toward the other end of the tunnel was more prominent.

Damn, how far does this thing go?

The further I went, the brighter the light became. I tucked the flashlight in my hand into my back pocket and looked above my head at the source of the naturally bright light. I squinted my eyes, looking up the cylinder-shaped hole above. The center of the brick lined cylinder was slightly unobstructed in its center, yet the light that beamed down was tolerable. Its brightness dampened by the all-consuming depth of the darkness.

"This is the well. The settlers built a tunnel from the Gallaghers cabin to the bottom of the well to seal it off. No well water, no settlement. The Dalys forced everyone to move."

I took another step to get a better look up at the interior lining of the well. A stone protruding from the layers of mud tripped me up. I fell upon a jagged cluster of sharp rocks. Pain went through my body on impact from both the rocks, and the holstered Corbin which jabbed into my side. I screamed in pain after my shoulder and the back of my head struck a blunt shaped rock behind me. As I lay on the moist ground, grabbing my aching shoulder, my head throbbed in pain. The fabric from my shirt was torn, and blood trickled from a cut in my flesh. I pulled my hand away and stared at my blood-soaked flesh. My focus was shaky as my vision blurred in the sunlight peering down the forty or so feet from the top of the well.

When my vision came into focus, I noticed an odd, oval-shaped bulge in the moistened mud protruded. The sight of the odd shape was unlike anything I'd seen that may have naturally occurred. I grabbed the edge of the would be rock, and pieces of brittle, layered mud fell from it.

I continued to peel away the flakes of mud until I saw the symbols carved into what appeared to be some sort of handle. A crescent-shaped moon was carved on each side of the circular shape in the center. I pulled on the handle and wiggled it until the firm grip of the earth relinquished it. The craftsmanship of the five inch blade attached to the handle was old and appeared handmade. The carved symbols were familiar. As I turned over to sit up, the top half of a human skull stared back at me, only the ocular cavity exposed, and the rest buried in mud. In the deeper corner of the open area at the bottom of the well, the milky white eyes of another corpse stared back at me. This one was different from the partially buried bones stacked underneath my feet. The body was still relatively fresh, probably a result of the bitter cold, wet, and inhospitable environment it rested in. Covered with bruises, her limbs were grotesquely broken, and she had a large laceration across her throat. It was the darker skin tone that left little doubt who she was.

"Oh, my God. This must be Ms. Jones. This is why we never found you. Hunted and murdered. Just like Hannah. These aren't stones. These are bones... No one ever removed the bodies," I mumbled.

I made my way back onto my feet and placed the blade into my pocket as I made my way back through the tunnel. The sound of my heart thumping in my chest and my boots dragging along the wet rock did little to distract me from the shooting pain along my side and shoulder.

The pain from the cuts and bruises from my fall annoyed me enough without the difficult dredge of the slippery incline of the walk back.

It left me no choice but to use my free hand to support myself against the filth and web-covered wall of the tunnel.

God, I hope a spider doesn't crawl across my hand or up my arm. I don't need any more to deal with.

"Jackson, you there?" I yelled out, in the direction of the subtle light a couple of dozen yards above me.

"Still here, Auntie Nola. Everything is good up here. Just waiting for you," he yelled back, his voice in the distance.

I continued the trek. The throbbing of my ankle swelling caused discomfort in my boot. For a few brief moments, my labored breaths were the only sound to fill the tunnel. It was only a few brief moments. A subtle hissing sound started behind me and grew louder.

"Trespasser." The voice hissed.

I turned to see where it came from. It sounded as if it was right next to me.

"Where are you?" I asked. My voice trembled from the combination of pain and cold.

"Tresspasssserr."

Inches from my face, the sight of its pitch-black skin and milky white eyes sent chills down my spine. Its hair fell past its cheeks and enhanced the sight of its sharpened teeth. The hissing sound grew to a wailing cry that rivaled any emergency siren on an ambulance rushing through the streets of the city. Its hair blew back away from its face from the force of the sound.

The pain from the reverberation of the scream in the tunnel disoriented me. I stumbled backward. Its claws sliced through my thigh and knocked me off my feet. I screamed in pain. I pulled Corbin from my holster. The flashlight fell from my hand and rolled away from me. The entity stepped toward me as I aimed at its chest. I fired four rounds into it. It screamed after the bullets ripped through its flesh and scurried away, back toward the well opening, and climbed up.

I hurried to my feet; the pain I felt just a short while ago was almost nonexistent as the adrenaline pushed through my veins like a raging fire feasting on a forest. My chest rose and fell with labored breaths. After I made my way back to the makeshift ladder, I looked up and gazed upon the youthful face of Jackson looking down at me with a nervous smile. His flashlight beamed down and partially obstructed my vision.

"Did you see it? I heard the scream and the gunshots." Jackson's voice was shaky.

I struggled to lift my injured leg. I used my arms and other leg to make my way back up the ladder. The adrenaline was no longer effective as I grunted with every climb of the ladder. The spiders were the least of my concern. I climbed out of the dank darkness of the tunnel and briefly lay on my back with my arms stretched out against the cold, splintered wooden floor. I struggled to catch my breath. The pounding in my chest mimicked the violent beating of a drum. As I reached up for Jackson's outreaching hand, I slipped on the blood on the floor that poured from my leg. After I finally made it to my feet, I pulled Jackson by his hand and led him out of the cabin.

"I heard the wailing and the shots. Did you hit it?" Jackson asked.

"I hit it—not sure if I hurt it, though. I think the silver had some effect on it. At least enough to scare it. We need to get out of here," I said, limping and grimacing in pain.

"You scared me, Auntie. I thought I lost you, too. My father is laying out there dead, and I thought I was alone. I was terrified. When I saw your face, I was relieved."

"Jackson, don't worry about it. I know there is a lot going on for you right now." The frigid air no longer felt like an assault, but an exhilarating relief when we stepped outside. The banshee was nowhere to be found.

"Look, I need to get back to the car and get something to tie off this wound. Then we need to get back to the house. I found something down there. Something big is my hunch. Let's try to reach the sheriff again, and get your father picked up. We have a lot to talk about."

"Yes, ma'am."

CHAPTER 22

I couldn't help but squint my eyes at the unforgiving brightness of the sun. The contrast of the darkness in that tunnel to the open field of the settlement was jarring. The sight of my brother-in-law's pale corpse as he still lay on the ground was sobering. I glanced over at Jackson, his back turned toward his father, unable to stomach the sight of him.

I know it hurts, nephew. It's a pain that's inconsolable. Don't let it fill you with the same rage and contempt as it did to me.

Sick of the ringing in my ear, I ended another call to the sheriff.

"Still no answer by the sheriff. Jackson, I'll call the sheriff's station and see if I can get one of the deputies so we can get your father picked up. Stay with him, Jackson. Stay with your father."

THE WALK into the Dalyville sheriff's station was like entering the somber environment of a funeral. Deputy Westin sat behind the large U-shaped front desk and spoke softly into the phone, while Deputy Shannon sat not too far away, his head firmly supported by the hand on the desk. Although Shannon and I had our differences, my instincts told me that he'd be more open to questions about what the hell was going on with the sheriff.

"Hey, Deputy, thanks for picking up your phone earlier and getting the coroner out to us. I hated for Jackson to see his father laying out there like that," I said, clutching the bloody, makeshift cloth bandage on my leg.

"No problem. I'm just doing my job. Besides, no boy should have to see his father like that. How is he holding up, anyway?" Deputy Shannon nodded in Jackson's direction, who sat near the front door.

"Kid is stronger than he looks. Much stronger than I was at his age, and I didn't go through half of what he's gone through over the past few days," I said.

I limped over to the chair behind me to rest. The room spun a little. The blood loss must have been more than I thought.

"Nola, that leg seems to be a lot worse than what you're letting on. I'll grab the first aid kit."

Deputy Shannon walked behind the desk and grabbed a brown packaging box tucked away underneath. He set the box down in front of me and knelt down by my side. I never realized how gentle his eyes were. They were soft as if he sympathized with the lives lost in his town. Maybe Shannon wasn't so heartless after all. He reached into his back pocket and pulled out a pearled colored folded metallic object that looked like it might have cost him a decent amount of money. With the flick of his wrist, the blade popped up. "Stick your leg out, and whatever you do, don't move. I know it don't look it, but this blade is as sharp as a razor," he said, quickly pouring the some of the fluid from the bottle of alcohol rub over the blade and cutting away the fabric of my pant leg and exposing my wound.

I flinched and bit my bottom lip.

"Why were you guys out there? Were you hunting that thing and took the kid with you?" Deputy Shannon asked as he removed more medical supplies from the box.

"No. Unfortunately, his father ran out of the house once he overheard what I thought was going on here. We tried to catch up to him and chase him down, but it was too late. It had already... It had already killed him," I said, my voice trembling.

"He didn't die like the rest of them. Why is that?" Deputy Shannon picked up the brown bottle and poured the antiseptic on my leg. The liquid fizzled and bubbled.

"I'm not sure. Maybe it was being territorial. When I went in, it attacked me too, but the silver rounds I had scared it away or affected it somehow," I said.

"Silver?" Deputy Shannon inquired; his brow curled in confusion. He held up the bandage wrap after he inspected the three large lacerations across my thigh.

"Silver has the natural properties that are often adverse or deadly to things... unnatural," I replied.

"Ah... I see. Sounds like a supply that can be hard to come by and costly," said Shannon. He wrapped up my wound tightly twice over. "That's gonna need stitches. Until you can get it done, keep it clean and wrapped. No blood thinners," he said. Shannon sounded like some sort of medical professional. Far from the first impression of what I had of him.

"It has its challenges. To stay on the topic of deaths that were different from my sister, were you able to retrieve the other bodies from the bottom of that well? It obviously wasn't killed by that banshee, not with the number of bruises on her body," I said.

"We were able to retrieve the body. It was Ms. Jones, from best I could tell. I've seen her a couple of times, since she and that other lady showed up. I haven't notified the others yet. You were right about the other bones as well. The coroner couldn't get to those yet. Those will take more work."

"Thank you, Shannon. It feels much better." I stood and looked around the station once again.

"I want to apologize about the way I acted toward you before. I ain't got an excuse. Sometimes I'm just an asshole, I guess," Shannon said with a smirk.

I gave a smile in return. "I appreciate that, Deputy."

Jackson still sat on the bench by the door. Deputy Westin still whispered into the phone. I watched intently while his lips moved, and his words passed into the phone's receiver. The deputy paused his conversation and glared at me as I watched.

"Is there something I can help you with, little lady?" Deputy Westin asked.

"I'm no lady, and I'm damn sure not little," I replied. "Where's the sheriff? Has anyone been able to get in contact with him? What are you doing to find him?" I asked, staring back at him.

Deputy Westin hung up the phone, stood, and took a couple of steps toward me. Deputy Shannon stood in between me and Westin in response.

"I've been to his house, and we've been calling all morning. We've got nothing. No sign of his car, and his place is all locked up. It's almost as if he left town. Given the way some of the folks of this town have left, I can see him doing the same. I can't say that I blame him either," Shannon said, shrugging his shoulders.

Westin continued to glare at me with his cold and unforgiving eyes. I never noticed before, but his eyes lacked empathy, or any emotion, for that matter. Hell, I came through this door with a bloody stump for a leg and he couldn't be bothered to get out of his chair. His hand rested upon the butt of his holstered gun, as if he wanted to free it from its leather prison. I stared back.

"Is there something I can help you with, little fella?" I asked, a slight smirk on my face, as I moved the front end of my coat to display the butt end of Corbin.

"Motherfucker." Deputy Westin's blood-filled face turned him the color of a strawberry. I backed away from the desk to ensure I had my feet in position and watched him as he moved closer. Deputy Shannon once again stepped in.

"Easy there, Westin. Trust me when I tell you, you don't want to do that. Everybody, let's just all calm down," Shannon said.

"Shannon, he's the sheriff of this town. I'm sure he hasn't deserted you. At minimum, you need to kick in his door and take a look around inside his home. I haven't been here long, and even I know Sheriff Alfred isn't that type of man. I'm sure you know that as well. So, act like it, Deputy."

Shannon's eyes glazed over, fixed in my direction. His eyes came back into focus as he looked away in shame. His glance went back to Deputy Westin, and he nodded.

"Westin, let's go to the sheriff's house and see if there were any signs of a struggle or signs that he left town. We need to do our jobs, and make sure ain't nothing foul has happened to him."

"Shannon, look, that's a good idea, but I just got off the phone with the mayor. He's made me acting sheriff until we can have a special election," Deputy Westin said.

He smirked with a look of satisfaction. His hand no longer rested on his gun, but at his side.

"You? You've only been on the job for about a year. Why the hell would he make you—"

"T-this is what the mayor wants. If you have a p-problem with it, then give him a call," Westin stammered. "Besides, we have much more important things to do than look for some deserter. We need to stop the exodus of citizens, and make sure they feel safe. That's what the mayor wants, and that's exactly what we're gonna do."

Shannon and I both stared in disbelief. Deputy Westin stood there with his chest puffed out, along with a smirk that a person would have if they just had the last word in an argument.

"Let's go, Jackson. We need to get home. There is a lot to talk about. We need to invite some company."

I pulled my cell phone from my back pocket and limped out the door. Jackson trailed behind me as we left the sheriff's station. His cries were silent as tears fell from his bloodshot eyes.

"Charles, glad you answered. I need you and Tammy to meet me at my sister's house. There have been some developments. I'll text you the address."

The brightness of the television clashed with the warm orange hue that emanated from the fireplace. That fireplace was one of the few comforts in the hell I'd been in since I stepped foot in this death cesspool called Dalyville. With the clashing luminescence and the sunlight that peered through the living room window, it provided a well-lit room in an otherwise dreary environment. The loss from this house alone smothered the atmosphere with silence and grief. The background noise of the television did nothing but help distract me from constant thoughts of Janice and Darrius. If my focus veered to them, I could miss something, and the distraction could cost me my life, or even worse, Jackson's.

"How's it going, Auntie Nola? Did you come across anything new in that binder?" Jackson asked as he sat on the couch next to me. His face was expressionless as he leaned on the arm of the couch with his elbow and rested his head on his fist.

Although his eyes focused in the direction of the television, he didn't seem to pay much attention to what was going on. I'm sure his thoughts were focused elsewhere. We make quite a pair. Orphans born in the worst possible way.

"Nothing new, Jackson. Just trying to make sure I didn't miss anything." I placed my hand on his shoulder and forced a smile in his direction, unable to conjure any true happiness. "I'll find this thing. I'll find it again, and I'll kill it," I said, no longer smiling. My hand remained firmly on his shoulder, hope he benefited with a slight feeling of comfort from the human contact as I did.

"I think I'll go to my room and play some video games. I already grabbed some snacks and stocked up in my room, so I may be in there a while. Don't worry about me."

"Yeah. S-sure. Go and have some time and clear your head. I'll be here if you need me."

Jackson had the right idea as he retreated to his room and locked the door behind him. Normally, it would worry me, but his reassurance that he was okay seemed sincere. It convinced me that he just needed more time to himself. His youthful face and upbeat tone were a convincing combination, against my better instincts.

I'm sure he just needed some time alone to blow off some steam. It was a long day, for the both of us. Only a few moments passed after he closed the door and I heard Jackson's faint cries from his room. My stomach twisted in knots. My eyes welled at the sound of his anguish, but my hands trembled with anger.

For the first time since I arrived here in Tennessee, the thought of the soothing, burning pleasure of a stiff drink forced its way through my mind. It would help me deal with this blistering rage I needed to release. Before I managed to find the courage to scour the house for alcohol, the doorbell rang.

I hurried over to the door, anxious to see the expected guest on the other end. As I opened the it, the large, chiseled frame of Charles centered the entrance way. His fitted navy-blue long-sleeved shirt hugged his arms and firm chest, he accented with a fitted knit skullcap. He was lightly covered in snow flurries. The manner in which he carried himself left a presence in any room he entered. Tammy followed closely behind him, dressed considerably warmer in a body-length hooded coat. Her cheeks and the tip of her nose were as bright as red candied apples.

"What's the deal, Charles? It's not cold enough for you out there?" I asked.

"I run a little warmer than most," he replied. His tone void of emotion and he pointed his eyes toward the floor as he walked by.

Why won't he look at me?

"Thank you for meeting me here. I think we have a lot to talk about." I said as I closed the door behind them to spare myself any further exposure to the bitter, cold air.

"Your voice sounded panicked over the phone, and you said you have some information you wanted to share?" Charles replied.

"Yeah, Nola. What's going on? It's been frustrating sitting around knowing that thing is out there. I refuse to believe it's

Ms. Jones," Tammy said, removing her oversized coat that swallowed her tiny frame.

I pointed to the couch, offering both of them a seat. I stood in front of the fireplace after feeling the quick assault of the cold air from the opened door.

"I wanted to get you up to speed on everything that's happening. We need to keep our voices down because Jackson's in the back. He's resting and, most likely, grieving," I said.

"Nola, what's going on exactly? Why did you call us here?" Charles asked. He stood after brief stint on the sofa.

"My brother-in-law ran out to the settlement in anger behind my sister. I supposed he thought he could hunt that banshee on his own. He died last night. I don't want to go into the details, but Jackson has now lost both of his parents in less than a week's time."

The stunned look on both Charles and Tammy's faces mirrored the shock I struggled with. I couldn't prevent the deaths of Jackson's parents or mine.

What good am I, really.

"We found a tunnel that went deep underground and eventually led to the well in the center of the settlement. Charles, I found your mother's body down there, along with this dagger and the skeletal remains of others. On my way back, I had an encounter with the banshee, and it was definitely wearing your mother's face. I don't think the banshee is her per se, but I do think it's using both her blood and essence to manifest the witch's desire for revenge."

"Wait a fucking minute! Is that how you tell me my mother is dead? What the fuck is wrong with you?" Charles yelled. His eyes welled with tears as he fell back on the sofa.

Tammy bellowed at the news of the loss of her former boss. Her eyes filled with tears, as she placed her head in the palms of her hands.

"I know that news was hard to hear in such a direct manner, but I think we all knew this already. We just didn't have a body," I answered. I exhaled sharply, and my brow curled at the sight of both Charles and Tammy's tears.

"I don't care if we thought we knew or not. You don't get to be so cavalier about it," Charles said.

A sizable vein running across the center of his forehead protruded and throbbed. Charles scowled at me. Still in my hand, I clutched the dagger from the well tighter. A little nervous that there was a good possibility he could become enraged and violent after the news. I did. Not sure if that was the right response, but it was my response and it could be his.

My brow tensed as I felt the repercussions of my actions. For some reason, the thought of causing hurt to Charles was an unacceptable action for me, and for the third time since the news of my sister, I watched as someone received the news of the loss of a loved one, a parent no less. This time it was dealt by my hands onto another. Another burden I didn't want to carry.

The surprised vibration of my cellphone in my pocket distracted me from the tension in the room. The bright screen again displayed an odd message 'unknown caller.' I curled my eyebrows, staring at the screen.

Usually, there's a number. Whoever it was, I didn't have time for them right now. I tucked the phone back into my front pocket and left it to go to voicemail. My attention back on my guests.

"Charles, you're right. I'm sorry. I didn't mean to be so cold about it. I'm truly sorry."

Charles' gaze softened as he leaned back on the sofa; his large shoulders slumped. Tammy soon followed, wiping the tears away from her face with her hands.

"I need to talk to you two. I have more pieces to the puzzle than I initially said, and I'm hoping you might clarify a little more. When I first found out about your mother being here, Charles, I wondered, why this town? There are other towns that Ms. Jones could have acquired. Why Dalyville?" I asked.

"I suppose you received the file I left with your sister," Tammy interrupted. "I worked for Ms. Jones, closely for a little more than twelve years now. She was the smartest person I had ever met. For as long as she had an idea for this type of project, it was always this place.... this town. She kept an eye on this town for a good long while." Tammy pushed her glasses back firmly on her nose with her finger. "Probably longer than the time I've worked for her."

"I had a suspicion it was you that left that file. Charles came to town after I did."

Charles sighed after he looked up at me, as if he was irritated by my line of questioning. He stood and walked over to the fireplace. The smell of his aftershave was intoxicating; as his shoulders gently brushed up against mine when he passed.

"My mother knew all about the history of this place. The forbidden love between the settler and enslaved girl. The rape of that same girl by her master, and the contempt and hatred of Hannah by the mistress of the house, who forced the selling off of the baby from that rape. My mother knew about the murder of Hannah's oppressors and her eventual lynching as a result." Charles moved away from the fireplace and stood near the edge of the sofa. His toned softened when he continued to speak. "My mother did her research because she always does her due diligence on large acquisitions and projects, but this place was special. This place was where her great ancestor was ripped away from his mother and laid the foundational roots for our family."

"Charles, are you saying the child that was sold—"

"Yes. My mother was born not far from here in Nashville. My grandparents moved to New York when she was a child. They couldn't stand the fact that Dalyville was thriving at the time. They knew what happened, and they made sure they taught their child her history. My grandpa was researching the family tree and found the bill of sale recorded in the state archives. The child was sold from the Gallaghers to another enslaver whose last name we now carry... Jones," Charles answered.

"Ms. Jones showed me the file I gave you. At first, I couldn't understand why she showed it to me. I think she just wanted someone to share it with. When I saw it, I understood what she was doing. She wanted to make it all right. That's what this was all about. Ms. Jones wanted to turn a tragic history into something positive, something beautiful and something powerful for her family," Tammy said, with tears falling down her face.

"I understand. Now I know why it chose her. There had to be a connection. I found this at the bottom of that well." I placed the dagger on the coffee table in front of me.

The newly cleaned dagger sat upon the table. The curved silver colored blade and white marble handle reflected the flickering flames from the fireplace. The handle was engraved with the etching of two crescent-shaped symbols and three stars triangulated near the base of the handle.

"At the bottom of that well was death incarnated. Not only did I find your mother, Charles, I found several skeletal remains encased in mud and this dagger. My guess is that there were at least four bodies down there: Ms. Jones, the Gallaghers, and Hannah. This dagger belonged to the young Daly girl. She used this dagger to etch these symbols into the interior lining of the brick of the well," I said, handing both Charles and Tammy the impression I took at the well. "The symbols you see are often used to show a bind between two parties. In this case, it was between Hannah and Fiadh Daly. The symbols are also strengthened with a blood bond. I'd have to imagine that was the bond that sparked it all. Although I'm not sure how this dagger ended up at the bottom of that well."

"The Dalys," Tammy said.

"I'm sorry, the Dalys?" I squinted my eyes in confusion.

"Not the ones of today. Fiadh's parents. They killed her when they found out about who she was. Ms. Jones told me. Fiadh brought shame upon the family. Being gay and in love with a slave sent them over the edge. The father murdered his own daughter and dumped her down that same well, with his wife's support. Stabbed her with that dagger and left it in her. They were monsters."

"Christ, that makes five brutally murdered in that well, all before Ms. Jones."

Tammy sat up attentively near the edge of the sofa. She straightened her back as she finally unbuttoned the top of her blouse as a result of the heat from the fireplace. "A blood bond? So, if I'm understanding this right, the fact that both of the young girls were brutally murdered in the same spot as their blood bond was done, it caused some sort of… reaction?"

"Yes, something like that. The witch made the well sacred to them. The desecration of their love triggered the bond and perverted it to a spell of vengeance. The murder and dumping of their bodies in that spot caused a volcano of wrath that bubbled under the surface. Until the death of Ms. Jones caused it to erupt, manifesting the monster that killed my sister and so many others."

"It was her blood, wasn't it?" Charles interjected.

"I'm sorry," I replied.

"It was my mother's blood that caused the eruption. It's because we're descendants of one of the lovers. Do you think that was the eventual trigger?"

"It's more than likely, Charles. When it erupted, it brought all of the rage and pain of everyone down in that well with it. What's out there is wearing your mother's face, but it's not your mother. It's all love, mutated and perverted into pure vengeance and evil. The only questions we have left are who killed Ms. Jones, and how do I kill that monster?"

After she listened to everything, Tammy stood. Her hands trembled and her eyes welled.

"Ms. Maor, do you mind if I rest here tonight? I'm terrified to go back out there," Tammy asked.

"Umm... yes, that's fine. There's a guest bedroom down the hall. It's the second door on the left, past the first bathroom. Please try not to make much noise. Jackson should be resting. After everything he's been through, he needs as much peace as he can get."

"Thank you. I won't be any trouble. I just don't want to go back out there tonight."

Tammy quietly made her way down the hall. She somehow managed to open and close the old door with barely any noise at all. Charles remained on the sofa with his head down and shoulders slumped. He appeared to gaze at the dagger, stunned at all he had heard.

"Charles... Charles," I repeated his name unable to gain his attention.

His eyes were void of any response as I called out his name several times. I hesitated before slowly walking to the sofa and sitting beside him. My mouth opened several times, but the comforting words in my head refused to fall from my lips. I managed to wrap one arm around his broad shoulders, gently encouraging him to rest his head upon mine. His headstrong will relinquished as he rested his head. His brief yet subtle sob was unexpectedly interrupted by the ear-splitting wail of the banshee in the distant night air.

The next morning, I awakened and clutched my thigh with both hands, grimacing in pain. The bleeding had stopped, mostly, but the pain and soreness was relentless throughout the night. After I redressed the wrapping on my wound, I limped my way to the kitchen. The nutty aroma of the fresh brewed coffee enticed enough endorphins for me to produce a smile as I entered the kitchen. Both Tammy and Charles were already up and sat at the kitchen counter talking, as they drank coffee. The somber looks upon their faces made it obvious to me that they were still trying to process our conversation from the previous night. A quick glance near the coffee table in the living room confirmed the dagger was still in the same spot after I left Charles asleep on the sofa.

I didn't take him for a man willing to show vulnerability, no matter how brief. It both caught me off-guard and opened me up a little. I could empathize with his pain, and maybe one day,

I could return the favor and share a little with him. Now wasn't the time.

"Good morning, Nola," Charles said. His tone was dry and his face was without emotion.

"Good morning, Charles. Good morning, Tammy," I replied, averting my eyes away from him and trying to focus on Tammy alone.

"Would you like some coffee?" Charles walked near the pot and grabbed a mug.

"Sure, but we need to make it quick. We have way too much to do today. God willing, we'll live to see it all through. Where's Jackson?"

"He never came out of his room. Hasn't really made a peep all night that I'm aware of," Tammy replied.

"JACKSON!" I yelled, with panic in my voice.

The sound of a door opening in the hallway was quickly followed by the irritated tone of the sighing teenager that made his way into the living room.

"What the hell do you want?" Jackson answered. His brow curled, with parsed lips, and balled up fists.

"Relax, kid. I wanted to make sure you were awake. Look, I know you've been through a lot, but I need you to do me a favor. I want you to pack a bag for a couple of days. Take only the necessities and only those items that can protect you against the darkness. Something you can sneak past airport security. We don't have time to waste. I need you thousands of miles away before nightfall," I said in a stern tone. I patted Jackson on his shoulder. "Tammy, I need you to take Jackson back to New York and stay safe until all this is finished. Take the nearest flight out and leave as early as you can... today."

"Why? I'm not going anywhere," Jackson protested.

"Oh, yes, you are. This isn't a negotiation. Get in your room and pack your shit. I need you safe. I'll let Tammy fill you in on everything when you two are on your way to the airport."

Jackson stormed off to his room and slammed the door behind him.

Tammy stepped toward me with her hand on her forehead in concern. "Nola, I know you're the hunter here, but what happens to Jackson if you don't... if you don't make it?"

"Let's hope it doesn't come to that," I mumbled.

"Sounds like you have a plan, Nola," Charles said.

He left the kitchen counter and headed toward me. His white tank top hugged his firm frame and my eyes lingered longer than I expected. His powerful arms and smooth sepia skin were an enticing combination of temptation.

"Well, I'm sure we all heard the wailing last night. That only happens when it hunts. We need to find out who or how many people it killed last night. As far as I know, the sheriff is still missing, so we need to find him. Most importantly, we need to find out what the Dalys know about what happened to your mother and what's going on around here. I don't expect to get much cooperation from anyone, so it might be a little sticky today. Are you up to giving me some back-up? I'm sure the military taught you something," I asked Charles, while he stood there with a smile on his face.

"Oh, Ms. Maor, you have no idea what I'm capable of,' Charles replied, the smile evermore present.

"Perfect. Let's go and make some trouble."

THE USUALLY CALM atmosphere of the Dalyville sheriff's station was overtaken by the multiple ringing phones. Deputy Shannon stood behind the large U-shaped desk, built about three feet higher off the ground and, most importantly, obviously built to make others feel more fear than safety. Deputy Shannon slammed the receiver down from his current phone call and refused to answer another blaring phone.

"Goddamnit! This is ridiculous. What do you two want?" He blinked rapidly; his breathing was labored.

"Looks like you could use a little help around here. Where are all of your cop buddies?" Charles asked, while staring at Deputy Shannon with a spiteful grin.

"Have you found the sheriff yet? What's going on, exactly, Deputy?" I asked.

Deputy Shannon glared at me with a look of contempt, while he continued to answer the never-ending barrage of ringing phones.

"Look, we didn't find him, but since you're a former police officer, I'd love to have your help. Families are fleeing the town and

I don't have any help with the evacuation or anyone around to talk them into staying. I don't know where Sheriff Alfred went. Maybe that thing got him, or maybe he turned coward and ran." Deputy Shannon shuffled papers around in front of him. Shannon glared at the constantly ringing phone next to him.

"Deputy, you and I both know that the Sheriff wouldn't abandon this town. I just met him, but his sense of duty was evident. What I do know is that we could use his spirit right now. I think things will get worse before they get better. Maybe it's best the townspeople leave."

Deputy Shannon stared at me with an absent expression look on his face. Hope wasn't present in his eyes. The slow, sober infestation of defeat crept in. "The sheriff is gone. Westin is God knows where, and there is a monster stalking and killing townspeople. Now, you're here to tell me things will get worse?" Deputy Shannon asked rhetorically, shaking his head.

"Hey, deputy! I just wanted to drop in," a bearded, flannel dressed man shouted from the sheriff's station doorway. "We're on our way out of town. Too much shit is happening around here, but the diner—" his voice trailed off. "The diner looks weird. Someone had pulled the plywood off the door, and it looks like somebody went inside. I thought you should know. Be safe, deputy. Hope you aren't dead if… I mean, *when* we come back." He exited the station laughing inappropriately.

"Nola, please. I could use your help. I have no one to go out there. Please, help me out," Deputy Shannon begged. His attitude was a far cry from the cliche' arrogant law enforcement officer I encountered only a couple of days ago. He answered the still ringing phone beside him.

"Not a problem, deputy. We'll check out what's going on over there, but after that, all of our efforts will go toward finding the sheriff, and getting answers from the Dalys about what the hell happened here. Agree?"

Deputy Shannon nodded in agreement as he continued his conversation. The ringing from the other available lines continued.

AFTER CHARLES and I pulled up in front of the diner, I noticed the already weathered plywood had been removed from the shattered door, and the frame was lying on the ground. I covered my nose with my hand at the stench that permeated from within. The brightness of the mid-day dimly lit the interior of the diner enough to illuminate the disarray inside. The turned over tables and chairs, along with the three-prong scratch marks deeply sliced into the floor and along the walls presented as if two brawling bears had made their way inside.

"My God, what's that smell?" Charles said, with his brow curled in repulsion.

"Death," I replied.

"I've smelled death before, Nola. This is different. This is...rot."

I stared at Charles as the look in his eyes appeared distant, like he was lingering on an unpleasant memory. Charles walked deeper inside, through the double-swinging doors into the kitchen, where the smell intensified. The growth of mold spread from the still lingering dirty dishes near the sink to the countertop. The trash was filled with maggots that feasted on the rotten garbage inside and also covered the trash can crawled along the outside.

"Nola, look." Charles nodded his head toward the walk-in deep freezer.

"Jessie?" I said.

A trail of one hundred-dollar bills led to the propped open deep freezer door. The withered, gray-skinned body of Jessie lay at the foot of the entrance. Black sludge which poured from her eyes, dried to her skin. Her arms were wrapped around a five-gallon peach bucket, now filled with assorted denominations of money.

"Last night, when the banshee wailed, it was coming here... for Jessie. Why take vengeance on her? She seemed so sweet," I said.

"The stench in this place doesn't make sense. Even with the garbage, the mold and poor Jessie there, the smell of decayed flesh is overpowering. Something isn't right," Charles said. His jaws tensed at his assertion.

"The diner lost power, Charles. I'm sure they had a freezer full of meat that's rotted in there."

Charles stepped around Jessie's body and glanced into the freezer.

His stare lingered inside the freezer. His mouth was agape, and his eyes widened. Charles' hands began to tremble, and his chest rose and fell rapidly.

"N-Nola!"

I quickly walked toward him and looked inside the freezer. The sight of the carnage within sent pains throughout my stomach. The nausea built inside me, and the pressure to maintain control became too overwhelming. I leaned over as vomit spewed from me and tears fell from my eyes. Inside, several rotted and swollen human torsos hung from meat hooks that dangled from the ceiling. Multiple severed legs and arms from a variety of people were wrapped in brown butcher's paper and stacked on the shelves along the wall. The shoes of the victims remained on the dead feet of the severed appendages. A folded letterman jacket sat on the floor in the corner of the freezer. Next to it sat a young woman with frozen blue skin, who only wore black French cut panties and a letterman jacket.

"Oh, my God! The missing people. The diner. That hotel. They used them for food. It's the fucking stew!"

CHAPTER 25

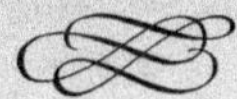

Charles and I were mostly silent after we ran out of the diner into the safe confines of the car. We could do nothing but stare at each other in disbelief. The fresh cold air was a welcome change from the stench. I reached into my front jean pocket and dialed the Dalyville Sheriff's station. The length of the ring on the other side of the line felt as though it was a suspended moment in time. My thumb continuously tapped on the steering wheel as the only display of panic that manifested itself outward.

"Dalyville sheriff's station, Deputy Shannon speaking." His voice, on the other end, seemed irritated and short of patience.

"Shannon, this is Nola. I need you to text me the Dalys' address. I need to talk to them immediately," I said, my tone uncompromising.

"Usually, the answer would be no to such an obviously out of line request. I've been on the phones all damn day with scared townsfolk leaving. There isn't much of a town left now, so giving you the mayor's address really doesn't matter anymore," Shannon said.

"I suppose still no word from the sheriff?"

"No, Nola. Nothing. What do you want with the Dalys?" Shannon asked.

"You need to get over here to the diner or send Deputy Westin this way," I said.

"Westin is still out somewhere helping the mayor with something. What is it? Only God knows. At this point, if you think the Dalys are up to no good, then my hunch is Westin knows about it too."

"Of course, he is. You'll see for yourself real soon. The Dalys' hands are dirty. They played a part in everything that had happened in this town. I plan on finding out why. My advice, whenever you get over here and see what you need to see, burn the fucking place to the ground."

I hung up the call, and my phone dinged almost instantly from an incoming text. Charles glanced over at the screen and read its details.

"243 Churchfield Lane."

"Well then, let's go and have a conversation with the Dalys." I turned the ignition and my foot slammed on the accelerator.

～

As we pulled up to the Dalys' rather large and cheerful pastel teal home, I couldn't help but shake my head at its aesthetic. The house sat out like a sore thumb and screamed misappropriation of funds from the small-town mayor. On top of it all, Deputy Westin sat on the front porch, feet propped up on the railing, accompanied by a shit-eating grin on his face—the perfect, depraved look considering the dark souls he seemed to protect.

Before I could fully put the car in park, Charles opened the passenger side door and stepped out of the car. His large frame moved at a pace with a purpose. His shoulders squared and his stride just as wide as he made his way to the base of the front porch. I'd seen a lot of athletic men move before. Quite a few 'roided out freaks that had something to prove. They would jump out of moving vehicles and drooled at the thought of putting their hands on what they classified as a suspect, warranted or not. This was different. Charles moved with a natural confidence and a step that only fell into the category of someone that was special. I wasn't sure if it was military training or just his natural ability, but he was a very capable individual who had my attention.

After bringing the car to a stop, I quickly exited and caught up with him, tapping my side with my elbow to ensure Corbin was holstered.

"Deputy Westin, I see you've made yourself comfortable over here. Are you working an authorized detail by the town or are you just working as the Dalys unofficial shit brigade?" I asked.

Charles stood next to me at the base of the front porch stairs. Westin continued to stare out in the direction away from us. His body language refused to provide the reaction I sought.

"Westin, have you seen the Sheriff?" I asked, noting the smug expression on his face.

"I don't know what brought you and that fella 'round here, but ain't nobody here seen that sumbitch," he replied.

Westin spat the disgusting fluid from his chewing tobacco into the cup in his hand. He didn't get it all inside. The rest dripped down his chin, which he quickly wiped away with the back of his hand. An absolutely repulsive habit if I had ever seen one.

"We need to talk with the mayor and his wife. I know they're home. They've been cowering inside their home since things fell apart around here. Tell them to step outside?"

Westin continued his slow and methodical chew, again spitting into his cup as his eyes diverted away from us. I quickly made my way up the stairs and onto the porch, standing next to Westin. His gaze still averted.

"Are you a deputy or not? People are dead or missing, and the Dalys know what the hell is going on."

"Little lady, I don't know what you think you know, but this is what I *do* know. You and that buck over there are gonna get back in your car and get the hell out of here. If you don't, then maybe sometime soon there will be people looking for you, just like you're looking for that snowflake sheriff." Deputy Westin leaned back on to the rear legs of the chair he sat in and spat into his cup once again, again slightly missing as the slimy brown liquid dripped from his chin.

"I'm about out of patience with you, asshole. I told you before, I'm not little, and I'm damn sure not a lady," I said with a slight grin.

I kicked the chair from under him. Westin fell onto the sturdy wooden floor of the porch. I pulled Corbin from its holster and pointed it at his head. The look in his widened eyes excited me as I bit down on my bottom lip, begging him to move. Charles made his way up the stairs and stood in front of the doorway as it quickly swung open.

Mayor Daly stepped outside with a rather large handgun. His shaky older hands struggled to hold up the barrel-heavy Desert Eagle, and he did his best to point it at Charles' head.

"Look, you two spooks. Get the fuck off my property before you end up buried with your sheriff friend in my backyard," the mayor said, as he was finally able to point his heavy handgun at Charles.

Charles looked Mayor Daly in his eyes. The rage was recognizable within him—I had seen it so many times within myself—but his stare was almost primal. Charles' reflexes were fast as he grabbed Mayor Daly's hand holding the gun and struck his elbow, the sound of his bone snapping mimicked that broken dried up tree branch. The gun fell to the floor of the porch. Mayor Daly screamed out in pain and fell to his knees. Charles struck him in the jaw with his massive fist, as he then fell to the same wooden porch as Deputy Westin. Charles quickly retrieved the semiautomatic handgun from the porch floor and pointed it at the mayor.

"What the hell do you mean buried in your backyard; you piece of shit?" I yelled, striking Westin jaw with the heel of my boot.

Blood and chewing tobacco spewed from his mouth and onto the floor.

The unsettling laughter of the mayor as he clutched his arm in pain was almost in sync with the deputy's laugh. The mayor wiped his mouth with the back of his hand.

"You think I'm gonna let some outsider come in and buy up this town? That bitch had to die. Strung her up and buried her in that well. And that do-good sheriff who I trusted that didn't know his place? Well, I buried his ass in my backyard. My wife's flowers should be beautiful next spring." Mayor Daly's laughter mirrored that of a madman. "This is my town. You and your friend here are gonna share their fate."

"You sick fuck," Charles yelled. "What about the diner? All of the bodies!"

"Everything is a resource. Those goddamn kids coming here and using our town as their personal party toilet. This place is hurting, and the Dalys are providers." The mayor said as he sat up with his back against the wall, clutching his arm. "It's too bad we didn't get a chance to get a buck as meaty as you in that pot."

Charles swung the back of his hand at the mayor and struck him across the face. The mayor's laugh was silenced as he looked up at Charles with contempt.

"Well, now you've got that banshee punishing all of you. It wears a really familiar face, and I'm sure it'll be your way soon," I said.

"No damn monster is gonna run us off our land. All of those other cowards might have run off, but we ain't going nowhere. My advice to you is to get the hell out of here before we make you part of our next pot of stew."

I watched as Mayor Daly's obnoxious laugh spilled from him and his eyes cut toward the window. My eyes followed and watched the edge of the double-barrel shotgun begin to lower and take aim.

"Charles, look out!"

Charles dove away from the window and Mayor Daly as the person on the other end of the shotgun fired. I holstered Corbin and leveraged my hands, then leaped over the porch using the banister railing. I landed on the grass below. The drop provided a significant amount of pain from the ground as I landed. Pain reverberated from my thigh throughout my body. I quickly made my way to the car. As I looked over my shoulder, Charles wasn't far behind. We made our way into the car, and I started the engine.

"Get the fuck off my land!" Mrs. Daly yelled, firing once again from the porch, hitting the car and shattering the rear passenger side window as we sped off.

"Charles, we need to get back to my sister's place and get every weapon available to us. We haven't seen the last of the Dalys, and on top of it all, the banshee is still out there."

CHAPTER 26

I pressed down on the accelerator. The car sped down the long country road away from the Dalys' house. I reached for my cell phone and once again dialed the sheriff's station. The phone rang for what seemed like a ridiculous amount of time.

"Pick up the goddamn phone, Shannon!"

"Sheriff's Department, this is Shannon."

"Shannon, this is Nola. Have you been to the diner yet?" I asked, yelling with panic in my voice.

"Nola, it's only me here. I haven't been able to step foot outside of this place all day. I don't know—"

"Shannon, shut up and listen to me. You need to watch your back. Westin is working with the Dalys. They're psychopaths. They killed Ms. Jones. They killed the Sheriff, and they are fucking cannibals. You're not safe. You hear me? We have to work together on this if we want to survive the night," I pleaded. My heart thumped in my chest. "You need to get out of there. Shut the station down, and get over to my sister's house now!

"Are you kidding me right now? That's a lot of wild accusations. To be honest with you, it sounds ridiculous. I've put up with you only because the Sheriff thought you were useful. Well, he's not around anymore, is he? Monsters and cannibals terrorizing the town and running everyone off? A murderous may..." Deputy Shannon's voice fell silent on the phone.

"Hello. Shannon, are you there?" I moved the phone away from my ear and glanced at the screen to ensure connectivity.

"Mayor Daly, what brings you this way, sir—" the sound of gunfire cut Shannon short. The violent rattle of the phone on the other end caused my heart to thump violently in my chest.

A vaguely familiar voice on the other end of the call spoke. "Is this Nola? Where are you, sweetheart? You guys left in a hurry, and we weren't finished with our discussion. Look you're a guest in my town. I'm concerned about your complaints. Let's have a meeting and we can discuss your issues. How's that sound?" The creepy laugh that followed his shallow words disturbed me. I could feel his bad intentions ooze through the phone.

I quickly ended the call and glanced over at Charles. He grabbed his right shoulder and winced. I rolled my eyes and exhaled deeply, frustrated at his wet crimson colored shirt.

"What the hell, Charles? Were you hit?" I asked.

"I'm fine. I've been through a lot worse. What the hell happened on the call?"

"It looks like we're on our own. They got to Deputy Shannon, but I have an idea to bring all of this shit to a head."

I eased off the gas pedal and pulled into the town's only gas station. The darkened interior was a bit of an unusual sight in the middle of the day. Whomever the owner was must have decided to leave town like the others who'd rather stay alive than protect pieces of a town already dying. I picked up a nearby cinder block and tossed it through the locked glass door. The glass shattered and crunched under my feet as I made my way inside. Charles exited the car, still clutching his shoulder. Blood trickled down his arm as he followed me inside.

I grabbed three of the five-gallon gas cans from the far end shelf inside the convenience store and flipped the switch on the fuel dispenser master control. As I made my way back from behind the counter, I noticed Charles gathering first aid supplies, along with water and beef jerky.

"Get your ass back in the car. Once I fill these containers, we're heading to the settlement. Are you sure you're okay, Charles?"

"I'm fine. It's mostly a graze. I told you; I've been through much worse. That wasn't hyperbole, Nola. Just get the shit you need, and let's burn this motherfucker down," Charles said with a wink and a sly grin.

A fleeting smile snuck onto my face. I turned my head so Charles wouldn't see. I hadn't met many men like him. Not in the police department and definitely not any of the time I've been doing this on my own. Most of them were fun for a short time. None of them I would have ever considered as a partner. Charles was different. He was a little vague about his past, but he was smart, strong, confident, and a leader. Charles was someone I would want to spend some time with in the future… maybe. After I filled the last of the three containers, I placed them in the trunk and sped off with Charles in tow, along with the absolute will to cause chaos and pain on the evil that has infested Dalyville.

THE TIRES of the car ripped through the light brown, winter weakened grass. Trail marks were heavily imprinted from the gravel road to the front stairs of the center structure of the settlement. Charles and I both grabbed a gasoline filled container from the trunk of the car and hurriedly poured it onto each porch. The pungent smell of the gas burned my nostrils as it mixed with the bitter cold air. A trail of gas poured by both me and Charles led from the porches of the settlement, which eventually merged to a single trail and led directly to the well. I poured the last of the gasoline from the container in my hand over the brick structure and down into the well.

I ran back to the car and drove it to the start of the gravel road, then retrieved the last gas container from the trunk. The heat from my breath turned into a thin white cloud as I exhaled into the frigid air. The record cold snap of Tennessee would have run me out of town under normal circumstances. Not this time. These weren't normal circumstances. I felt nothing. Nothing but the anticipation of the radiant shimmering flames I was about to unleash upon this ungodly piece of land. I grinned as I franticly poured the gas on and around the brick of the well, emptying more than half of the final containers' contents into the bottom, with a trail dripping down the interior of the brick. I threw all three containers down inside the well, imagining the hard plastic hitting the bottom and bouncing off the protruding bones of the victims beneath.

"Well, that's everything. Let's light this baby up," Charles said with a grin.

I took a step back and exhaled heavily one more time, pulled the lighter from my pant pocket, and ignited the edge of the well in front of me. The flames spread rapidly down and around the well, then away from us, branching off and slithering through the grass like a snake, and ultimately burning and consuming every structure in the settlement. The flames grew wildly and tore through the decaying wood like a juggernaut. Heat rose from within the well. The sound of the splintering wood under the extreme heat was a pleasure I had not seen in fifteen years.

Just look at you, Nola. Bringing the light once again. The source of all this death, the cause of so much pain...Let it all burn.

"Maybe we get lucky and this fire cleanses and kills the banshee as well, just like it did for James," I mumbled.

"Who's James?" Charles replied.

"A soul who opened my eyes to everything around me. A soul I wish I still had with me today. Let's get back to the house. One way or another, we might get company tonight. We need to prepare the best we can for it."

Charles and I watched as the flames consumed a small part of the past that would live on through pain.

~

As we walked back into the confines of my sister's home, the frigid air tried to make its presence felt inside. The flames dimly lit within the fireplace were on their way to burning themselves out. Charles reached for a poker and placed a couple of more logs on the fire. Focused, I hurried to my sister's study to gather a few things I thought we would need. Banshees were new to my hunt. The lore I knew only focused on the origins, but killing it was something that moved me into the realm of the unknown. Janice's small arsenal, collected to fight the supernatural, was well supplied. I laid out a variety of guns and an assorted variety of blades. All outfitted with silver in one form or another. It helps when the federal government can provide the funds for the arsenal.

My run-in with that thing in the tunnel had its drawback, but it was not without a little beneficial information. It almost took my leg off, but the silver hurt it. The blades were of a variety of lengths and were either silver-plated or pure silver. The bullets for the guns followed the same technique.

Not long after, Charles followed behind me. His eyes widened at the sight of it all. The rows of books and weapons would be plenty to shock a novice exposed to the world of hunting.

"I know this can all be a little much, Charles."

My eyes never cut in his direction. I focused on filling Corbin with the silver bullets it needed and lining the newly attached slots on my belt with as many back-up rounds as I could fit.

"No time to waste. Grab something you're comfortable with. They could show any second."

Charles picked up the hunting knife mounted on the wall beside him. He twirled it effortlessly in his hand and slid it back into the holster he held in his other hand.

"Like I said, I'm not new to any of this. Give me the sawed-off double barrel. Regular rounds will do. I don't need the silver, but I can back you up," he said.

No silver?

"Are you hiding something, Charles?" I said with a flirtatious grin.

He chuckled at my accusation. "No, I just have some humans as my top targets right now. When the time comes, I'll grab whatever is in here that will help with our supernatural target. Right now, all I can think about is putting down those redneck assholes that killed my mother," he replied.

A smile once again crept over my face as I listened to his macho bravado. I wasn't impressed by the words, but I loved the confidence he spoke with. The smile dropped from my face as I stared down at Corbin and spun the wheel barrel.

"Nola, can we stop a moment here? Look, I know we need to focus, but you do know it's okay, right?"

"Charles, what in the hell are you talking about?" I asked; my brow curled.

"The pain you carry is all over your face. You're burdened with it, and you don't have to keep it all in. I'm here. I'll listen."

"I think you need to stay in your lane, softy. I don't need you to help me deal with anything personal I might be going through. I've done just fine all these years all by myself."

"I doubt that very much. I've only been here a couple of days. I've watched you carry the burden of pain and loss for everyone around you. You haven't skipped a beat from what I can see. So, unless you aren't human, you can't continue to keep it all bottled in. You need to release it all at some point. I'm just saying... I have an ear if you need one," Charles said. His eyes locked onto mine.

I looked away and picked up the dagger found in the well. I turned my back on Charles and stared down at the dagger for what seemed like an eternity, then tucked it into my waistband. I reflected on what it meant to the two souls who used it to carve a symbol of their love into a well that was the center of their new town. A place that was supposed to be a land of hope and new possibilities for them. Instead, this town turned Hannah and Fiadh's dream into a nightmare. A place where they both lost everything. A place where I lost almost everything, too.

"Charles, let's just finish preparing."

"No, I don't think I will. I've lost my mother. She was everything to me. My father abandoned us before I was born. You've lost your sister and your brother-in-law, and God knows what else. It hurts, Nola." Charles put the knife down on the counter, slowly stepped closer to me and placed his hands on my shoulders. "It's okay. It's okay."

His massive, muscular arms wrapped around me and pulled me closer to his chest. He held me tightly, and from that point, for the first time in a very long time, I felt safe in someone else's arms. Tears fell from my eyes as I wrapped my arms back around him and squeezed tightly. A flood of emotions filled me. I felt human again, and I didn't want that feeling to stop. I backed away from Charles, only to lean in closer to satisfy my curiosity about the taste of his lips.

"Nola, no. That's not my intent. I'm not trying—" Charles said.

"Shut up. This is what I want, Charles. *You* are who I want right now. We may not live to see tomorrow. I just want to talk." My tone was soft, and my heart felt open again.

I pulled off my shoulder holster and sat down on the couch with Charles' fingers intertwined with mine. Charles laid across the sofa with his head resting in my lap. His eyes always locked on mine. I gently stroked the top of his head. The repetitive motion and the feel of his soft curly hair was soothing to me.

"What do you want to know?" he asked. His fingers rubbed the back of my hand.

"I'm not sure what I want." I shoved his head off my lap and exhaled.

Charles sat beside me, slowly shaking his head.

"Fifteen years ago, someone I thought highly of was consumed by the darkness. I lost him. I'm not sure what could have become of us, and I think about him often. The day he died was the first day I started to kill off pieces of myself to deal."

"Sounds like he was someone special to you. Why didn't you explore it more?" Charles asked.

"The same thing that happened here. A beast killed him and took James from me. From that point, I keep losing people close to me." I mumbled as my eyelids became heavy.

"We've both lost people. My mother is gone, and I never knew my father. No brothers. No sisters. I'm alone now, and the loss of my mother will hurt for a long time. She was all the family I've ever known," Charles said, lowering his head.

I lay my head on his broad shoulder.

"What you do is unbelievable. To be able to stand toe-to-toe with these vicious creatures, it would unnerve even the most hardened soldier. You do it, though. You do it, but now things are different for you. Nola, you have Jackson, and you two will need each other every step of the way."

The crackle of the fireplace was calming. The red glow of the setting sun peered through the window.

If this is my last day on earth, I'll make sure I get a good night's sleep.

Sleep, a restful sleep, it had avoided me for over fifteen years. The echo of the high-pitched wail in the distance violated the few moments of peace I managed. I opened my eyes and immediately stood from the couch, wincing from the throbbing pain from the wound on my thigh. The scream was prolonged and sounded angrier than before. The pace of my breathing increased. My hands shook from the shrill noise and the smothering inclination of death that accompanied it.

"Sleep will have to wait another night. We're about to have company."

CHAPTER 27

The blood-red hue of the low setting sun peered through the window just before darkness fell upon the sky. The surprising presence of snow flurries as they fell didn't invoke the joy it would have on a normal visit to my sister's place. My anxiety as the sun set lowered in the sky forced me to sigh heavily in anticipation of what was coming. The energy it took to stay dialed in through all of this was soul-sucking. It all needed to end, one way or another.

As I glanced over at Charles standing across the room, I watched him inspect the sawed-off shotgun he insisted was his weapon of choice.

"Thank you for listening to me," I said in a monotone voice, gazing into his eyes. "I hadn't opened up to anyone like that in a very long time."

"Same for me. Tammy is the only other person that knew about me never knowing my father. You were easy to talk to," Charles replied, still inspecting the shotgun.

It occurred to me that maybe Charles was worth the risk. My gaze lingered longer than I expected. Charles caught me in the act of admiration and returned my gaze with a smile of his own.

Another ear-piercing wail of the banshee occurred as the last of the sunlight was extinguished by the earth. The warning was anticipated. I expected our actions in burning down the settlement would enrage it and the Dalys in the most effective way possible. I held on to the slim hope that it would kill it. Not so lucky.

"The question now is, who is it coming for, and when?" I asked.

"I'm sure we'll find out soon enough."

As we both paced the living room, we were startled by the sudden blinding brightness of halogen lights and the obnoxious roar of a souped-up engine driving onto the lawn only a few yards from the front of the house. The light partially obstructed my view as it penetrated the windows and violated my sister's home. I could only make out a few human silhouettes inside among the shadows. The engine of the truck roared several times; its front end torqued as if it was a predator thirsting to pounce on its prey. Both doors of the truck swung open simultaneously, and all three silhouettes stepped outside.

"Charles, quick, kill the lights," I whispered.

I ducked down under the windowsill, eyes still affixed on the three familiar figures who now stepped in front of the truck's headlights. The deputy was still in uniform, another man with his left arm now in a sling, and the ratty-haired woman in their company appeared to be Jean Daly. All of them were armed with some type of gun in their hands.

"C'mon now, Nola. Don't be shy. Why don't y'all come outside and finish the conversation we had earlier?" Deputy Westin yelled. He had an apparent grin on his face and a rather large rifle, all easily seen, even with the assault of the bright headlights of the truck.

"Nola, do you see them?" Charles asked, his voice tensed.

"Shit, yes. Get down!"

A barrage of bullets tore through the wood and glass at the front end of the house. Charles and I laid on the floor of the living room; both arms partially covered our heads as the whizzing sound of passing bullets ripped through the air. Pieces of glass and particles of wood fell on us as bullets tore through the front of the house. The thunderous clap and muzzle flashes from the discharging weapons were similar to a fireworks show, but the feeling was far from festive. The disturbing sound of cackling laughter lingered under the ear-piercing blast of gunfire after its echoes trailed to a stop.

"You guys alright in there?" Mayor Daly laughed.

I pulled Corbin from its holster and crawled over the shards of glass to the window to get my eyes back on the makeshift Dalyville militia. Charles quickly followed with the sawed-off shotgun in hand.

"C'mon now, y'all, I promise we just wanna talk." Westin laughed once again. The mayor and Jean joined along with him.

"To hell with that, I wanna gut that bitch," Jean followed.

I peeked over the low end of the windowsill and watched the elation on their faces as they laughed. It echoed in the night's air. The smell of gunpowder and smoke was a complete contrast to the innocent sight of the snow flurries.

"Nola, look!" Charles' eyes widened at the sight of the creature stealthily approaching behind the Dalys.

Our eyes synced at the sight of the pair of three-pronged, elongated claws reaching out from the shadows. The black, stringy hair fell forward and covered most of its face. Only its dead white eyes and jagged teeth were still prominent. Its claws wrapped around Deputy Westin's head and snatched him off his feet, pulling him into the thick cover of darkness. The cries of the deputy echoed in the night as he screamed for his life, only able to push out a singular word.

"HELP!"

"Oh shit. What was that?" Mayor Daly shouted. The handgun extended in front of him shook as his hand trembled. He moved with timid footsteps as he moved closer to investigate Deputy Westin's screams.

"Jerry, what the hell are you doing? Bring your ass back here," Jean pleaded.

Mayor Daly paused at his wife's pleads and squinted his eyes, hoping to see into the thick, dark, tree line next to the house.

The banshee emerged. Its jerky movements quickened toward the blind side of the mayor, claws again extended.

"Honey, look out," Jean screamed.

The creature grabbed Mayor Daly by the throat, lifted him off his feet, and pulled him close to it. The fear in the mayor's eyes was clear and present, even in the depths of the darkness. The creature screamed once again as its tentacle like tongue slithered from its mouth and into the mouth of Mayor Daly, then latched to the back of his throat. His eyes turned black and liquified. His face sunk in, and his skin turned gray as it drained him of his life force. The banshee extended the mayor's body away from it and snapped his neck. It released his body, which fell limply to the ground. The beast turned its head and stared at Jean; its smile unnaturally stretched beyond human limits.

"No!" Jean yelled.

She raised her automatic assault rifle and pulled the trigger. A barrage of bullets tore through the creature. Thick black blood splattered from it as it stood its ground, unaffected. The claws of its feet ripped through the frozen grass as it dashed toward Jean. Its claws extended and cut through the rifle, slicing it in two. It pierced both claws into Jean's ribs, pinning her in place and lifting her off the ground. The banshee pulled Jean close and released its soul-sucking wail. Its tongue soon followed. Her attempts to scream failed and only led to gurgling sounds as she choked on her own blood, struggling to breathe. Her eyes turned black, liquified, and poured from her skull. Similarly, the banshee snapped Jean's neck and her gray-skinned, lifeless body fell to the ground. The banshee wailed toward the sky; its horrific facial expression still relishing in satisfaction. It turned and stared at us. The still burning headlights of the Daly's pick-up truck illuminated its boney limbs as they twitched violently.

"Nola, we can't stay here. We need a plan," Charles whispered.

"Yeah, no shit. You take that side of the room and I'll take this side. Make it have to maneuver to both sides to get to us. Whenever it turns its back, attack. You get me?"

"How do we kill it?" Charles asked.

The creature's claws ripped through the bullet hole riddled door and tore it in half. Its slender, tall frame took up the entire height of the doorway. The massive, elongated, black talon claws on its feet and hands were too large to fit through the door. Its sharp, jagged, shark-like teeth protruded through its lipless mouth as if it was ready to tear through our flesh.

"I have no fucking idea."

CHAPTER 28

The sight of the creature, so up close and personal, provided an unnecessary reminder of the close encounter down in the depths of that godforsaken well. Only this time, it didn't need to squat down to fit in a narrow tunnel. Its tall, slender frame filled the height of the door frame. Yet even with my experience hunting so many vicious creatures, the sight of it was repulsive. My breaths were rapid. My hands trembled while it stared at me and grinned grotesquely. The weight of my legs felt twice as heavy, and fear crept into every part of my body. My limbs trembled, but I persisted. The only goal was getting Charles and me out alive. I looked over at Charles and every part of his mannerisms was steady. He was an Army Ranger. Charles mentioned he'd been through a lot, but this differed from war. He told me earlier today that this would unnerve even the most hardened soldier.

That man does not look scared at all, I thought.

Charles stood across the room with his feet shoulder width apart. His hands firmly gripped the shotgun, and his focus remained squarely on the monster in front of him. I felt more at ease as I watched him. At that moment, I knew Charles had my back. The banshee's bones cracked with its jerky movement as it stepped inside. Its bird like clawed feet penetrated the floors, and the wood splintered at the assault of its sharp claws. The lights inside flickered. The banshee glared in Charles' direction, its grin wide and unnatural. The lights in the living room burned brighter and white hot, as the face of the creature was brilliantly lit. Charles's once stern and focused expression turned. His eyes widened and mouth agape as the face of his mother crept closer towards me.

"Charles, she's coming in my direction. Stick with the plan."

Charles froze as it moved closer.

"Goddamn it, Charles, that's not your mother. Remember, she's in the morgue. Wake up!"

I pulled Corbin from my holster, pointed it at the head of the creature, and fired, shattering the glass of the framed picture on the wall behind it. A loud bang followed and echoed inside. The beast slightly stepped to the side after the impact of Charles's shotgun blast. Black liquid sprayed from the banshee onto the nearby wall.

The creature turned and took a few quick steps toward Charles. I fired several of the silver rounds from Corbin. The banshee screamed in the familiar way it did down in that well.

It's definitely the silver, but it's not enough, or it's the wrong weapon.

The creature turned back toward me and wailed, a bloodcurdling sound that made my bones rattle. As I felt the icy blade press against my skin, I widened my eyes in surprise. Fear made me forget. I pulled the dagger from my waist and tossed it as best as I could to Charles. The banshee's dead white eyes focus in my direction.

"Charles, try this. Now!"

Charles reached out to catch the dagger; his hand slightly cut by the blade. He pulled his hand back and screamed in agony. The blade fell to the floor and slid across the floor and under the couch.

"Fuck!" I yelled. I fired the last round in the once loaded barrel of Corbin.

Charles gathered himself and fired the second shot from his double-barrel shotgun, hardly affecting the creature. He immediately followed his shot by running toward the monster, completely unarmed. As he moved closer to the beast, its long bony limbs reached out and ripped through his chest with its claws. Blood sprayed from his torso. He dropped to the ground, unconscious.

I dropped Corbin onto the hardwood and sprinted across the room. I slid on my stomach to the couch and reached under and grabbed the dagger. The creature spun back toward me, then sprinted in my direction. It lunged out with its claws, their bloodthirsty tips pointed in my direction, aimed for my head and eager to rip into my flesh. I ducked and spun on my knees in its direction, dagger in hand. With a swing of the blade, I sliced through one of the lower portions of the banshee's leg. It squealed as its blood sizzled on top of the dagger's blade. The creature swung its back hand and struck me in the ribs. The impact caused me to stumble and fall short, just in front of the fireplace. I leapt back to my feet and gripped the dagger tighter.

As I moved close enough, I jumped toward it and plunged the silver blade into the would-be heart of the beast. It screamed in agony. The vibrations shattered the only mirror mounted in front of the fireplace. The scream caused me to cover my ears with my hands as I fell onto my back. Blood trickled from my ear cavity. I quickly moved back onto my feet. With both hands, I pulled the blade from its heart, then plunged the dagger deep into its head. It continued its vicious scream until its dead eyes turned from the pearly white haze to the deep black color of onyx. The etchings on the handle of the dagger flashed a burning bright yellow. The beast glowed a blinding white light as its scream stopped. The banshee burst into nothing, sending a spray of its black blood all over the room. Silence followed.

I rushed over to Charles, where he lay unconscious on the floor, still bleeding profusely from his deep chest lacerations. I turned him over onto his back and revealed his blood-soaked shirt.

"Charles! Charles… wake up!" I yelled, gently smacked him in the face. "Please… Get up, Charles."

His eyes blinked rapidly before they opened. He smiled as he sat up, grimacing in pain.

"What the hell are you doing? Slow down, hero," I lectured.

"I'm okay, baby. That couch looks way more comfortable than this floor." He said, his breathing erratic. "Did you finish it off?

Did you get it?" He asked as he stumbled his way onto the more forgiving couch.

"Yes. We got it. I was right about the blade. By the way, tough guy, you dropped the damn blade when I tossed it to you. You're not built for this sport, are you?" I said with a smile. "Let's get you bandaged up. We'll address that 'baby' comment once you heal up a bit."

"That might be a good idea," Charles replied.

"Thank you for having my back. I'll grab the first aid kit," I said, resting his head on a throw pillow.

I rushed to the bathroom, stumbling on the way as I reached for the sharp pain from my rib cage. My leg still throbbed with pain. I grimaced and slowed, continuing to the bathroom for the first aid kit.

"Adrenaline wearing off. Guess that rib shot did some damage," I said with a slight smile, still relishing in my victory.

As I entered the bathroom, I opened the medicine cabinet and didn't see a traditional first aid kit in sight. So, I grabbed the necessary items to make an effective bandage for Charles. When I closed the cabinet, my reflection stared back at me. The scar on my face still prominent. Memories of my parents flooded my head. A family photo of Janice, Darrius, and Jackson hung on the nearby wall. It was an odd place for a family photo, but the photo was also odd. It showed all three of them squeezed into an airplane bathroom, taking a group selfie. I had no idea how all three of them fit in there and were able to get the door closed. The smiles on their faces were genuine. A true moment of happiness. The memories of my parents were now joined with the memories of my sister and my brother-in-law. The laughs we shared and the recent tough times we had been through. Tears pours from my eyes. Emotional pain erupted from my core and spilled out of me. I screamed in complete agony at the thought of losing all of them. I collapsed to the floor and just lay there as I wept.

CHAPTER 29

The bright sunlight the next morning was a welcome sight while I packed my bag and made all the necessary phone calls. The darkness always triggered discomfort or anxiety after the hunt. This case didn't make it any better, but I discovered a new appreciation for the cold when I found myself in the company of freshly fallen snow.

It was comforting.

Although I found a fondness for the cold and the snow, it wasn't home. Not my home. Getting back to New Orleans was my focus. There was nothing left for me to do here, at least for a while.

"Getting ready for a trip?" Charles asked. He stood in the doorway of my sister's bedroom, shirtless and leaning on one side of the doorframe. His bandages on his chest were still soaked with blood, but he moved well for a recently severely injured man.

"Well, aren't you the strong soldier? How in the hell are you on your feet? That's a nasty wound you have on your chest," I said; my brow curled and eyes squinted.

"Not bad. I clearly remember telling you on many occasions since we met that I was capable of more than you thought I was," Charles said in a sarcastic tone. "I didn't want to bother you last night. I heard the crying, but I thought you needed the time to get it all out."

"I did. Thank you for being so considerate. I have to go. I can't stay here, Charles. New Orleans is my home. I'm coming back next week to get the house packed up. Especially the research and weapons. I'll have Tammy send Jackson down to me there. There's no way I'll have someone else raise him." I went to the other side of the bedroom and continued to pack my bag. "I'm not sure if I'm up to it, but I'll do what I have to. You should know that I called my sister's old unit with the FBI. They should be here by tomorrow to clean things up the only way they can. Just tell them what happened, and you'll be fine. I've already given them the gist of the situation. They're aware of you and everything that has happened. It'll be your job to fill in the details. Do me a favor. Point them in the direction of that creepy old man at the motel. They'll connect the dots from there."

"Nola, why don't you and Jackson move to New York with me? I'm sure there are plenty of... let's say, unusual things happening there," Charles asked.

"No!" I snapped. "I know you feel as though we've been through a lot together, but the truth is, I know very little about you. Definitely not well enough to move my entire life to be with you. There's too much unfinished business in New Orleans. Besides, I'm not sure you're the man for me. I won't uproot my life and move to another state for a man when I have such an important job to do."

"Okay. Fine. You don't trust me. I'll be straightforward with you. My mother had a plan for this town. I'm going to see it through. With her passing, everything is mine now. We shared a vision. Except, it was a slightly bigger vision on my end. I'll offer you a fair price on this place, but I'm not leaving here until my mother's vision is fulfilled."

"I get it. You're doing everything you should to fulfill your mother's dream and do what needs to be done. I can't ask you to put that aside for me, even if I wanted you to. Which I don't. Maybe we can get together every now and then on the holidays or something? I'm not sure how much family you have left. You told me about your father leaving before you were born and you know it's only me and Jackson left, so—"

"I have something a little more interesting in mind. Let me take a couple of months and make sure this project is underway. Our company has a satellite headquarters down in New Orleans. We've done a lot of work down there over the years. Once I get this completed, I'll spend some time down there. I'd like to see where this could lead us," he gestured, his hand pointing between him and me—

"You're an extraordinary woman, Nola. Maybe our friendship can be nurtured into something more. Once I'm done here, Tammy can run the New York branch. I'll come down to New Orleans and expand that branch. If, that is, you'll make a little time for me?"

Charles smiled. His laughter caused a slight bit of pain as he clutched at his chest. His strength and charm were impressive, one of the things that drew me toward him.

"Deal! I won't make any promises on commitments, but let's see if you're a man of your word."

"I am. Let's see if you can show me more of what's deep inside you and more of what darkness is out there in this crazy world we live in."

"That's a deal. I guess I'll see you in New Orleans."

I walked up to Charles and gently place my hand on his side, then kissed him on the cheek. I grabbed my bag and left the ghost of my sister's once nurturing home. The snow started up once again, providing a beautiful sight of the snow-covered trees and roads that were so pleasing to the eye. It was time to find a new way in New Orleans.

As I DROVE the highway that led back into Nashville, I reflected on Janice and the things we shared. My sister was gone, but the person she was and the things she taught me would live on. The thought of her hard-ass demeanor and the love she nurtured her family with produced a moment of happiness and a smile onto my face. That was the moment I promised myself I would raise Jackson with that same deep nurturing love, along with a bit of that hard-ass demeanor.

Deep in thought, my cell phone rang again, vibrating silently against the leather armrest. The bright screen once again displayed the words 'Unknown Caller.'

"Who the hell is this?" I exhaled sharply after picking up the phone.

"Hello!" I answered with frustration.

"Hello, Ms. Maor. I've been trying to reach you for quite a while," said the deep raspy voice on the other end. "I've heard you've been busy."

"Who is this? If you need my services, I'm out of the office at the moment, but I'll be glad to talk to you in a day or two."

The voice on the other end laughed. "No, Ms. Maor, I don't need your services. I do wonder how that scar on your face has healed up? I remember so vividly when it was put there."

"What? Who the fuck is this?" I screamed. My knuckles turned white as I gripped the steering wheel tighter.

"That's not important right now. What is important is the amount of blood you've spilled of my kind. You've hurt my family, Nola. There's a reckoning coming for you, and New Orleans. Your parents were first. When we're done, you and your city will be nothing but blood and ash."

The call ended abruptly as the other end disconnected. I threw the cell phone to the floor on the other side of the car. I pressed down on the accelerator, the car engine revved as I rushed to the Nashville airport. The tension in my head grew while I replayed the words of the creepy voice on the other end of the phone call. I exhaled sharply, thinking about what was possibly coming for me. The words passed my lips as I gently rubbed the scar on the side of my face.

"The past never dies. It lies dormant and festers, until it's time for it to rear its ugly head. There's unfinished business."

End.

NOTE:

Nola, Jackson, and Charles will return.

ABOUT THE AUTHOR

Ashon Ruffins is a native New Orleanian and a military Veteran. He earned a Master's Degree in Business Administration, while also holding certifications for several other professions. He spends his days serving his fellow veterans as part of the daily grind. However, he loves the art of storytelling in all genres and believes the best lessons in life can be told through fiction. *It is the passion for telling captivating tales of horror and morality that gives him a fulfilling and well rounded life.* Ashon is also a huge mental health advocate.